Dagobert

Call from the Distant Past

Rita Traut Kabeto

Dagobert

(Call from the Distant Past)

Text and cover illustration Copyright

Rita Traut Kabeto 2012

ISBN 978-0-9635416-5-9

kabetofandr@gmail.com
http://sites.google.com/site/ritatrautkabeto

Dagobert

Part I

It was past midnight. I was lying in bed but could not sleep. My mind kept reliving the events of the past day, and each time I reached the point at which I rushed into Leon's open arms a shudder of delight went through my body and aroused me again and again.

We had not seen each other since that sunny spring afternoon of the previous year in Hanfurt. We had gone on his motorcycle to celebrate our birthdays with his family in the hill country, called Rhoen. On the way, we had stopped at the border between West Germany and Communist East Germany, a border that runs right through the Rhoen. A group of three East German guards patrolled it on their side while West German guards were watching from nearly invisible surveillance positions farther back. Russian-American relations were strained in nineteen sixty, and a border incident could provoke an international crisis.

The border was nothing more than a roll, a low continuous roll of barbed wire and beyond it a very broad strip of bare plowed land called no-man's land, and no one was allowed to be there. I had seen beyond the barbed wire a silver thistle, a low growing rare flower, and had asked the guards to pick it for me. When one of them invited me to pick the flower myself, I had no trouble stepping across the wire roll and walking onto Eastern territory. As I bent down to pick the flower I felt poking in my back. I thought the guard was having some fun with me. "Just a minute," I said, only to feel a more insistent poking in my back. When I stood up, the guard who had been doing the talking commanded me to start walking. He was pointing in the direction of East. I still thought they were joking. But when three rifles were aimed at me I got the message. I could hardly believe that they would actually take me prisoner. Nothing I could say made an impression on them. When Leon yelled at them to let me go, they told him to shut up. He had warned me not to do something stupid, and seeing me marched off into no-mans land he called after me that he would let my parents know what had happened to me.

Fortunately for everyone, not much of anything was to happen. The guards marched me to the nearest village whose inhabitants had been forcibly removed. One of the old farm houses had been turned into a guard post where the commandant questioned me at length about my parents, their political affiliation and the like. At my accusation that the guard had told me to get the flower myself, the commandant said, "is it your habit to obey orders from East German border guards?" I thought it was funny – until the expression on his face taught me that it was not funny at all. That's when I had begun to worry.

They kept me isolated in a locked room till dark, then put me in a jeep and drove me somewhere. There was no moon that night, it was pitch black. I was told to get out and start walking. I had no idea where I was, East or West, in a field or by a river bank. There was nothing else to do, so I walked, no struggled through weeds and underbrush, bumping into small trees, getting my face scratched by low branches, fearing to fall into a body of water or get chewed up by thorny brambles. When I saw a light in the distance I followed it and came to a farm on the West side of the border.

That was more than a year ago. I had not seen Leon since then – until yesterday.

It took a long time before exhaustion set in and made me fall asleep.

The spacious room I was renting was located on the first floor of a small villa on Linden Street in Muenchen, a metropolitan city with the easygoing character of the Bavarian soul. The house was surrounded by patches of neglected flowerbeds and shrubs, all of it contained inside a rusty wrought-iron fence. It had a gate to a short walkway that led to the entrance on the East side of the villa. Two wars and decades of poverty had taken their toll on the once decorative façade. It was now sooty, and the window frames were in great need of paint. My room had a separate entrance that led directly via a short stairway to the outside door. I had never had so much privacy and couldn't keep my face from breaking out in a broad grin every time I thought about it. Just two days ago I had still shared a room with my younger sister, Hildegard. There had been times in the past when I even had to share my bed. Mother had never stopped treating me like a child, despite the fact that I had turned twenty in August, had held the job of nanny to my sister Paula's twins, had worked in a medical clinic, and had been housemaid to Mother and nursemaid to my four younger siblings

Beside the very comfortable bed there was a night stand and on it a pretty little boudoir lamp with a shade of pink cloth and fringe all around the lower edge. A wardrobe and a table with two matching chairs looked like antiques from the previous century. Two large windows facing a fairly unobstructed East endowed my room with lots of light. My landlady was Frau Schuessler, an elderly woman who rented out rooms because she needed the extra income to help meet expenses.

When I woke up it was still early. Leon flitted through my mind again. Since I wouldn't have to be at the Academy till ten o'clock I pulled open the two wings of one of the windows, rested my arms on the deep windowsill and looked out onto the street. It was a beautiful sunny day in early September. The street was lined on both sides with large ragged old Linden trees that had just barely survived World War II and would perfume the air during next year's spring.

Watching the world go by had always been a relaxing thing to do. During my growing years adults had thought of it as an act of nosiness or laziness, something every self-respecting German housewife would take care not to overdo. Yet there was purpose in watching people – one might figure out from their appearance what profession they belonged to, or judge from their facial expressions if they were happy or not, and from their clothing how well off they might be, not to mention the hope that one might see a few good-looking young people of the opposite sex.

There was something mesmerizing about it - people walking by from left to right, from right to left and back and forth, and continued turning of the head created a kind of trance. Several old women, dressed in black, with prayer books in hand and heading in a common direction gave me to think that a catholic church was nearby where seven o'clock mass was being held. It seemed to be the old women's lot in life always to be wearing black or very dark gray or brown. They wore black as a sign of mourning for, perhaps, a husband; and before the mourning year was over some other relative would die and require another year of wearing black, and so, some women would be wearing black for the rest of their lives. It was as though their own lives were over, and there was not much for them to do but keep house, go to church every day and mourn. Thinking about them made me sad for I could easily be ending up the same way if I had not insisted on - no fought for - a professional career. I would be a governess, and that was the reason for my entering Muenchen's Pedagogical Academy. I chose Muenchen versus any other city because Leon was here. I felt light and gay at the thought that Leon and I could see each other every day now, if that's what we chose to do. No more hiding and lying and sneaking around, no more fear and anxiety about what to expect from Mother on coming home. I was free at last.

It was time to get dressed, and after using the bathroom that I shared with my landlady I took breakfast with her in her kitchen at seven-thirty exactly. She looked at me and smiled.

"Good morning, Frau Schuessler," I said.

"Good morning, Stephanie. You came in late last night," she said with a knowing smile.

"Did I wake you up?"

"Well, I heard you going to the bathroom."

"I'm sorry, but don't worry, it won't happen again. It's just that I haven't seen my friend Leon in such a long time. We had so much to talk about."

"Well, I'm glad to hear it."

I took a slice of bread - wonderfully fresh and fragrant bread. I sniffed it. "There must be a bakery nearby," I said with a glance at Frau Schuessler who smiled. "Were you already out just to buy fresh bread?" When she nodded, still smiling, I said, "and I heard you neither coming nor going."

"There's an exit on the South side of the house. So you enjoy fresh bread, huh? Oh well, that's the German way. Some day, if I don't feel like leaving the house you can return the favor. Meanwhile, enjoy."

Frau Schuessler brewed very good coffee but she had forgotten the cream. I went to fetch it. Near the kitchen window stood a small radio that was playing the Volga song from "The Tsarewitch." I knew this song and its sad lyrics. They expressed the awful pain and loneliness of my youth so well that tears would have come into my eyes had it not been for Leon. Seeing that we had the same taste in music, I figured that Frau Schuessler and I would get along well.

"By the way, do you know how to get to the Academy? What bus to take?"

"My friend Leon will take me; and he'll help me figure out how to get there by bus. I'm a bit nervous about my first day; but it's just orientation. Is there a store nearby where I can get what I will need for classes?"

"There's one close enough to go on foot. Let me know when you want to go and I'll give you the address."

"That's great. Thank you."

"And you won't be too shy to ask if you need something, right?" Frau Schuessler asked with a smile that gave me to know that she understood my temperament and accepted it gladly. She was a plump lady of perhaps seventy-five, and her gray hair that seemed to be very long was pinned up in what looked like a complicated hairstyle. She wore no make-up, but her complexion was still fairly fresh and showed few wrinkles. She had on a straight blue skirt that reached to the middle of her calves, and house slippers. And to my delight, Frau Schuessler wore a pink organza blouse. I had never seen an old lady wear pink, not to mention see-through organza, which required tasteful lingerie underneath. Like many widows, she wore two wedding bands on the same finger – her own and her husband's. He had died ten years earlier.

On the previous day, when I arrived via taxi from the main railroad station, we had talked about her house rules and what she expected from me. She would provide breakfast and lunch; for the evening meal I would be on my own. I could do my laundry in the machine that was set up in her spacious bathroom. No doubt it was a later remodel of one of the other rooms. She had given me a set of keys, one for the downstairs door, and one for my room. Father would pay my room and board automatically on the first of every month - that was the deal. But knowing how things worked, or didn't work at home, I could only hope for the best.

Leon honked for me around eight-thirty. I had been watching from the window and rushed out to meet him. He had a slightly stocky build, and in the past I had only seen him in suit and tie or butcher uniform. But on that morning, he looked very smart in blue jeans, plaid sport shirt and a leather jacket. As always, his face was meticulously shaven. His after-shave lotion was the same I remembered from our dance classes, when nervousness had made him step on my big feet, and his sweaty

6

hands had trouble clinging to mine, and how I had wished that my dance partner were taller than I. His thick, blond hair was as wavy as always, and where it emerged from the forehead it wanted to stand up, but Leon had nipped that unruly behavior in the bud by cutting it very short.

While he took a long, happy look at me, his gray eyes still agleam with the joy of yesterday's reunion, I wanted to fall into his arms again, be held by him, just held for as long as I liked. But women in black walked by on their way to nine o'clock mass, and I didn't dare make a spectacle of myself. Instead, we stood facing each other and just smiled while our eyes held each other's gaze.

I was not allowed to bring male friends to my room, so we sat down on the stoop. Leon pulled out a city map and a transit map, and we studied them together until we were sure of the academy's location and how to get there by bus. Then he gave the maps to me to keep.

"Say, what are you going to study there; I don't think you ever told me." He put his arm around my back, and his fingers played with my curly blond hair. "I like it short; it suits you," he said. "So tell me, what are you going to study?"

In the past, we had never talked about my career goals because I had none. My parents had made all the decisions, and not just for me but for my siblings as well. And since they had never brought up the topic, I had never been aware that I might have a right to have a goal for my future.

When I first met Leon he was a journeyman butcher with the goal of becoming a master butcher. He had accomplished it after coming to join his brother's butcher shop here in Muenchen. I had always felt uneasy about Leon being a butcher. Butchers kill animals.

"I'm going to be a governess."

"Governess, hm. You'll be teaching the children of wealthy families, and even travel with them?"

"No, not really. I used to think it was like that; actually, in the old days it really was. Rich people who traveled a lot, they needed someone to look after the kids, see? I would have loved to travel around the world, see lots of different places and people. But now, It's more like being an educator, not a regular school teacher but more like working in institutions like an orphanage, you see?"

"Oh, that's good. I wouldn't want you to leave town with other people."

"I can still go out of town," I teased. "I could take a job somewhere in Australia if you don't behave yourself."

Leon laughed. "Yeah, I guess you could. But then you'll have to take me with you."

"Only if you behave yourself. Otherwise, you'll have to stay with your brother."

"Oh yeah!" he shouted, laughed, and poked me in the ribs where I was most ticklish. Then he asked, "how long will it take?"

"Five years," I replied. All of a sudden, what I had never paid much attention to hit me like a ton of bricks: five years! Five years of studying, five years before I would be able to go to work in my chosen field. I would be twenty-five then.

"That's a long time," said Leon, and his voice trailed off as he stared straight ahead.

He'll be thirty years old then, I though, but stopped myself from thinking any further. We sat quietly for a while. Five years! It kept coming back to me like a haunting. If I had started right after graduating from the tenth grade, I would be almost finished now. Anger against my parents arose in me, resentment for never having been asked what I want to do with my life, anger and disbelief that my parents could be so indifferent, or so ignorant or selfish as to never consider my aptitude, interests and inclinations, even my entire future. How could they do that to me!

Leon must have guessed my thoughts; he took my hand and said, "I know. Your parents."

"Yeah – well, I finally grew out from under my mother's thumb, but you know, if for some reason I had to go live at home again I'm sure she'd try to control me again. It would be a constant battle."

"You need your own home," Leon said with a sweet smile and a look of expectation.

"You used to say that I should have my own four walls. I think you were trying to get me to move to Muenchen, didn't you?" I checked his face, and his sheepish grin told me that I had guessed right. "It seemed impossible then, like going to America - I know that it's possible and that some people go there, but I also know that I'll never get there. And yet here I am, in my own four walls. And oh, I just love it. Doing what I please, when I please, how I please. I never had so much freedom in my entire life."

"You see, you fought for your right and won. But there's something wrong with your four walls."

"What?"

"I can't come inside," he answered with a suggestive look in his eyes. I felt myself blushing, and a slight shiver went down my spine.

"But, you know, it's kind of interesting how things work out. If I had gone to school earlier I wouldn't have met you at dancing class."

"That's true, and I'm so glad we did meet."

"Maybe that's what they call providence." We mused about it for a while. "By the way, what did my parents say when you told them that I was kidnapped by the East German border guards?"

"Not much, really. Your father thanked me for the information and said he would contact the police. Your mother didn't have much to say, except she asked how we came to be there. I explained about our birthdays, and that we wanted to celebrate them together with my family. I don't think she liked that. Her eyes grew real big, almost threatening."

"Oh, I know those eyes. She thinks they're her best feature. But they are menacing to me. She has said on occasion that a mother has to be firm when she has so many children. But does she have to beat on us to be firm? Why can't she be firm and still kind. And your mother has even more kids than mine. What's your mother like?"

"My mother is the best. She'd never lay a hand on any of us. Sometimes, all she has to do is look at us with an expression of disappointment and we'd get the message."

"Wow! You're so lucky. Does your sister get along well with her too?"

"Sure. By the way, you might have seen my sister and never known it. She works at the downtown branch of the Savings Bank, in Hanfurt. You probably know it, don't you?

"We do business there. I'll have to look her up." And I thought about his mother and how someday, maybe, perhaps she might become my mother as well.

After a while he continued, "it's strange. I always thought I'd be married by now, or at least engaged to be married. And here I am talking to you about going to school." He didn't seem to expect an answer, and I was glad because I had none.

"Maybe we better get going," I suggested and he agreed. I went back inside to fetch my jacket and school bag. As I came out the door I noticed him watching me walking down the steps with an admiring smile.

"You look great in slacks," he remarked; but then you always look great. You're a pretty girl and I can't imagine you looking anything but pretty no matter what you wear."

"Even a potato sack?"

"I don't know about that. Put one on and ask me then," Leon answered with a laugh.

I was used to criticisms, not compliments, and long established insecurity wanted to annul Leon's compliment. I had to remind myself that Leon did not make empty compliments; he meant what he said.

"I like wearing pants. I had always wanted pants, or blue jeans. Maybe it's because I wanted to be a boy; or because of all the Wild West movies I've seen. I fell in love with the Wild

10

West, you know. When I was a kid, I wanted to be a cowboy. Can you believe it?"

"I'm sure glad you're neither a boy nor a cowboy," and he kissed me on the cheek.

He swung himself on his motorcycle and I got on it behind him, just the way we had done on the day we had gone to the border. But this time I didn't have to battle my full-flared skirt and two or three stiff petticoats. It had required deft management skills to tuck the back of the skirt under my butt and keep the front of the skirt from flying into my face. Today, I was wearing slacks, which I had never been allowed to wear except for winter sport. The color was anthracite gray with a faint plaid pattern in varying shades of black and gray. And I wore a lavender short-sleeve knit top with it. I was very slender, if not outright thin, and the pants fit like a glove. I had bought them on the last day before I left Hanfurt. I was ready. I put my arms around his chest, placed my face against his back and held on with tender passion.

It only took about ten minutes to get to the Academy that was located on Marian Street not very far from the inner City. It was a large building, or rather it seemed there were several buildings of various ages and architectural styles, and they appeared to be connected to each other. The building was surrounded by lawns, shrubbery, and some very tall firs - a park-like setting that I knew I would enjoy. Leon drove around looking for the main entrance. Lots of young girls were streaming toward the building and by following with our eyes we found the entry.

"I'll come see you after work. We're open till six. By the time I clean up and change clothes it might be seven o'clock before I get to your house, okay?"

I felt like sitting, just sitting behind him with my arms around him and my hands caressing his chest. I could have sat like that forever. But it could not be. With a sigh and a quick kiss on his cheek I climbed off the cycle and walked toward the building with squiggly butterflies in my stomach.

The course of pedagogical studies I would undergo began with the eleventh grade. Four years had passed since my tenth grade, so a lot of the girls who descended on the academy were younger than I, and it made me feel rather conspicuous. I had graduated from a business school that covered eighth, ninth and tenth grades. I had wanted to go there because I thought I would have fun in a boarding school. My parents never explained to me just what kind of school it was. And that my interests and inclinations might not be suited to business work did not enter their minds and was never discussed with me. Fortunately for me, though, I discovered much later that my parents' decision had played right into Spirit's plans.

After graduation I had become an employee - but not in Father's business. Mother had snatched me up as housemaid for housework and nursemaid to my younger siblings.

Upon entering what appeared to be the main building I looked for an office and went there to find out where I needed to go and what to do. The receptionist was very kind and helpful, and after looking through some papers and files she found my applications and all that had come with it. A few other girls stood around, apparently also new and waiting to be given instructions. We looked at each other, shyly at first but quickly feeling the bond of common experience. I had never been shy, and so I began asking their names and where they would live – in private quarters like mine, or in the academy's dormitory. An assistant cut short our overtures and took us to the assembly hall.

Ahead of me, a swarm of giggling, laughing, talking girls surged as one entity through the narrow hallway toward the assembly hall. Suddenly, the entity opened to allow for a nun to pass through. For a moment I thought I was looking at Sister Angela from the boarding school at Venusbrunn where I had spent three years. There was that same familiar garb, all black, her head wrapped in white with only her face showing. On her head she wore the same roof-like structure with the 'gable' on top and the sides coming all the way down to below her elbows, black on the outside and white on the underside. Seeing this familiar figure made me feel right at home because I had been very happy with the nuns at Venusbrunn. I would find out a little later that this Academy was indeed run by the same teaching order.

The assembly hall was filling up. We sat down in an area reserved for the new students. Pretty soon a nun – the administrator, we were told – appeared and welcomed us. Then she filled us in on the many rules and regulations, expectations and situations that would at one time or other involve us. The chairs we sat on were hard; my old nemesis, my butt, began hurting again the way it had done so often during my school years. I had never understood why the nuns always accused me of fidgeting, inattention or even indifference. Only much later did I realize that the bones in my behind must have been assembled the wrong way, and that was the reason for my discomfort and, consequently, fidgeting. - I tried hard not to.

When the assembly had concluded we went to our assigned classrooms. I found a desk with two chairs in the back where my height wouldn't obstruct some tiny person's view of teacher and blackboard. The classroom filled up quickly, and then a lay teacher came in. She was an unmarried statuesque woman in her early thirties with blue eyes and blond hair that was pinned up in a large knot on the back of her head. Miss Geisel, that was her name, exhibited a pleasant demeanor, and her ready laughter was quite infectious. My initial nervousness began to wane, but after hearing a long list and description of the materials we would need, my nervousness increased again. We were allowed to leave around noon.

After I had purchased the necessary papers for my schoolwork – books were being supplied by the school – I had some time to myself and went looking for the church that, I figured, must be very near. Churches are great places to think and I needed to think about Leon and me. I walked down Linden Street and saw several other small villas, some older than others, one shut up altogether. One of the villas had been restored. It had a balcony with a black wrought-iron railing that showed bits of gold paint. No rust there. Its surrounding grounds were well cared for with shrubs and flowerbeds, and a gravel walk surrounded the property inside a well-painted black wrought-iron fence. The last house on the block turned out to be the bakery where Frau Schuessler had bought the bread. I decided to indulge myself with some bread sticks sprinkled with rock salt and caraway seeds as soon as I had a chance. For now, I just wanted to find the church. From the bakery I turned right onto Chestnut Street, and just two blocks down I could see the church. When I got close I saw that it was a really pretty little building in neo-gothic style but, like Frau Schuessler's villa, it appeared poor and neglected. Its windows were of clear glass because the colored ones had shattered during the war, if not from a direct hit then from the shockwaves of nearby targets. To my delight, the door was open and I went inside.

It is a remarkable sensation when one leaves the warm, colorful, sunny street and enters the cool twilight and deep silence of a church; it's like leaving the world to visit the abode of the Gods. I sat down on the last bench in the back so that no one would sit behind me. But there was no one at all. I preferred being totally alone, even in a public place like a church; I almost demanded it, inwardly, as if I had a right to such a privilege, and indeed I felt that way. I feared, or suspected, that people would be able to read my innermost thoughts and prayers. Oh yes, right through my back, so it seemed to me. Being alone with God in a church felt like the ultimate luxury, as if I had him all to myself. Of course, if my religion had taught me well, I would have known that God is everywhere that I am. But that truth had been buried beneath so many doctrines and dogmas and reminders of sinfulness that I didn't discover it till much later in my life.

My mind wandered to my relationship with Leon. Since the border incident we had not communicated with each other – until my arrival in Muenchen. On my part, it had been false pride that had kept me from writing. By the time I had realized what a fool I was, fear of having lost him had tormented me. But Leon had known that I needed to learn a few things, grow up and become assertive in my relationship with my parents. He had waited patiently and had never stopped loving me. An overpowering feeling of love and devotion came over me. I couldn't have been more fortunate for having Leon in my life.

I had noticed a hint of disappointment in his voice when I mentioned that I would be in school for five years. Did he have plans for us? Did he want to marry me? It wasn't so long ago when I hardly dared to think of him as my boyfriend. And yes, I didn't want to wait five years before getting married either, but I hadn't even started a career. I couldn't get married and go to school at the same time; it just wasn't done. Could Leon wait five years? Would I be able to wait five years? Wait for what? Oh dear!

I sat and thought and thought, enveloped in the silence of that little church until I was at peace again. There was no need for answers now. Time would show the way. And through some miracle of nature – or providence –

I was quite certain that it would be so.

When Leon honked for me around seven o'clock that evening I went out to meet him, free of doubts and free to be in the here and now.

"You look happy," he said.

"I am happy. I love you and you love me. What more could I want?"

"You are more beautiful than ever when you're happy," he said and pulled me close. He looked at me with a hint of yearning in his eyes. "But you still want something," he added teasingly. "Dinner, right?"

"Oh yes, you're right. I am hungry. Will you take me out?"

"Sure. But first, take this inside and put it in the refrigerator. You can eat it later." He pulled a package wrapped in light paper from his motorcycle bag and handed it to me. I opened it and found several long skinny sausages in it.

"I like those a lot. They go great with pea soup or lentil soup. Thank you Leon. I'll be right back."

I ran inside and stowed away the sausages and mentioned them to Frau Schuessler, so she wouldn't think that they were hers and eat them. At her age, one could never be sure that memory functioned well. Then again, if her memory did not function well, she would not remember that I told her not to eat the sausages. Drat!

Leon took me to a Gasthaus that he knew had good meats because they bought them from the Kramer meat market. In dancing class we had learned appropriate manners for interactions between the sexes, between old and young, and between higher and lower social status. Leon had been a good student. He was a perfect gentleman; he opened the door for me, let me chose the table and pulled out my chair for me. Then he sat down opposite me and encouraged me to order whatever I liked and not to worry about the price. That's when I realized just how much Leon referred to me in everything. It's as if he knew no other pleasure than to please me. Yet it never seemed to be a matter of giving in to me, or giving up his own preference. He never made a long face or grumbled about anything to do with me. He was just happy to do what I wanted or asked for. And this remarkable man was mine. It was sheer overwhelming to discover it. There must have been something different about my face, because Leon asked, "What are you thinking?"

"I just realized how very special you are," I said, a little self-conscious because I had not learned, and therefore had no practice in giving such straight-forward compliments.

He took my hands into his, leaned slightly forward so his face was close to mine, and he whispered, "whatever special thing you see in me is there only because of you."

It didn't take long for me to settle into a regular routine. I enjoyed my classes even though the technical jargon for child psychology and development was new to me and required some effort at memorization. Music and art I had always enjoyed;

16

French and English were not new to me and I was glad to be able to continue with their study. English, especially, was considered world language, and even traditional oldsters had discovered that understanding English was useful knowledge to have.

Leon and I spent a lot of time together; we'd go to the little neighborhood church, St. Andrew's, for Sunday mass, drive out into the country in the afternoons, sometimes on motorcycle, sometimes by train or bus, depending on the distance we wanted to go. We'd stop at a Gasthaus and have a cold sandwich – Leon knew a place that served excellent Schwartenmagen, his favorite sausage. He and Father had that in common. Leon liked his beer, and I had apple juice. At other times we went to see a movie, and once we attended a play. Neither one of us understood what was going on though, and even discussing it afterward did not help much.

I came from a family of eight, but Leon had me beat: he came from a family of eleven – ten boys and only one girl. His family had been among the many refugees that had been chased out of Germany's Eastern regions by Russians, Poles, and Czechs. His stories about their long trek through winter weather, walking or riding carts and wagons, with babies and frail old folks were an education for me who had never experienced any physical hardships. The Kramers had settled not far from Hanfurt in a small village in the hill country. Opportunities for jobs had been few, and Leon had to settle for an apprentice position with a butcher.

During October, a month that is dedicated to the Virgin Mary of the Rosary, we often went to evening services. We enjoyed the luxurious display of flowers, the smell of burning candles, and the emotional music of the season. Other times, we simply walked and talked. One day, Leon surprised me with tickets to the operetta Die Fledermaus, and we talked and laughed about the Viennese shenanigans in that story for a long time afterward. Some days I had to stay home and study for exams, or write lengthy papers for the purpose of which I

17

wished I had brought a typewriter. On Monday evenings Leon stayed home and went to bed early because he had to be at the slaughterhouse at four on Tuesday morning, where he and all the other butchers took turns getting their meats. They killed animals.

Frau Schuessler mentioned one morning at breakfast in mid November that she had not yet received the rent check from my father. I cringed. Now I would have to call home and find out what's holding up payment. Most likely, I would have to talk to Mother, and that still made me nervous. I thought I had become stronger, and more sure of myself, but perhaps that was all in my head. Old habits are hard to break, and my body just might react the way it had always done – with panic. Then again, perhaps Hildi would answer, and I was always glad to talk with Hildi, my sweet little sister who had a sixth sense. That evening I asked Frau Schuessler's permission to call home.

"I'll pay for the call, of course," I said.

"Yes, go ahead."

She went to the living room and I headed for the telephone that was located in the hallway. I was shaking as I dialed the number. Totally free, I was, huh? I realized that old habits were hard to break. It was around seven in the evening, and I knew that everybody would be at home now. It was indeed Hildi who answered the phone. "Fanny! Is that you? Oh, I missed you. When are you coming home?"

"Hold your horses, Hildi. Yes it's me. Are you okay? Do you have a good housemaid?"

"Yeah, she's okay. And she hasn't run away yet, so I hope that she'll stay a good long time. I like her. And the boys like her, too."

"You see, I told you you'd be alright. Now listen, so that this call doesn't get too expensive, let me talk to Dad. And say "hi" to the boys for me. I'll be home for Christmas for sure. And maybe I'll even bring Leon with me."

"Great!" she shouted, then put down the phone, and after a short while Mother picked it up. "Fanny? What do you want with Dad?"

"Hi Mom. Frau Schuessler hasn't received the rent check yet. Is it on the way?"

"I don't know anything about it."

"Well, could you ask Dad if it's in the mail?"

"He went downstairs to the office again. I'll ask him when he comes upstairs. How are you coming along with your studies?"

"Fine. I get good grades; as a matter of fact, I just got an A+ in child psychology."

"That's good. Now we better keep it short or it gets too expensive. Does Frau Schuessler allow you to use her phone?"

"Yes, she does. And I promised I would pay for the call."

"Alright then. Good night."

"Good night – and don't forget to ask Dad."

When I entered the living room, Frau Schuessler was reading the television program. "Do you like Opera?" she asked. "They're showing The Barber of Seville tonight."

"I'd love to see that, but Leon is coming for me pretty soon."

"Do you have plans?"

"Not really."

"Then why don't you ask him to come in and watch with us."

"You mean that?"

"Of course."

"Gee, I wish you were my grandmother. I never had any, you know. Well, of course I had two grandmothers like everybody else, but I never knew them." She laughed, and I went to my room to wait for Leon's honk. When it came I went outside and asked him to come in and watch the opera with us.

It was dark outside, and cold. It had rained most of the day and the streets were wet, soggy, mushy, and slippery from all the dead leaves on the ground. I no longer rode with Leon on his cycle after he once slipped on just such a soggy street and nearly rolled over. That moment of intense fear had forever imprinted itself not only on my mind but my body as well.

"You can meet Frau Schuessler; she's a very nice lady. It was actually her idea."

Leon agreed. We stopped for a moment in the dark stairway, and Leon put his arms around me, nuzzled my face, and then he kissed me tenderly and passionately. I totally got caught up in that kiss, and when we stopped, Leon said with a slight moan, "Fanny, my dear sweet Fanny, we need some privacy so we can talk. Will you come to my place?"

"Right now?"

"No – but soon."

"Sure," I said, delighted that he felt the same as I. "Come on, let's go in, it's almost time."

"Hello, Leon," Frau Schuessler said as she shook Leon's hand. She stood for a moment and looked him over. Her smile seemed just a little bit self-conscious, the way a young woman would look with pleasure at a handsome young man.

"You don't mind my calling you by your first name, do you?"

"No, not at all, Frau Schuessler."

"Good."

"Where would you like me to sit?" he asked, looking around at the living room. A settee and a couple of club chairs with a low, round table between them were arranged in such a way that the television, that stood between the two windows, could be seen from each one.

"Why don't you and Fanny take the settee. And Fanny, go and get three wine glasses from the cabinet over there while I get a bottle of wine."

"Oh, please, Frau Schuessler, don't bother yourself about us," Leon said.

"It's no bother at all. I enjoy having company. Don't have it often enough." She looked indeed happy; I hadn't seen

20

that expression on her face before now. I took out the wineglasses from her cabinet that stood against the wall near the window. An oil painting hung above the cabinet; I had never noticed it before. But the scene it depicted seemed awfully familiar to me. It showed the ruin of a fortress atop a wooded hill, and much of the walls had crumbled except for one tower that seemed pretty much intact. Extensive woods all around the ruin and far into the distance showed the way Germany must have looked a long time ago. I couldn't shake the feeling that I knew this place.

And then I remembered another time when I had that same feeling. It was in Venusbrunn on one of our longer hikes, when we came to the fortress ruin Wildenburg that had also crumbled except for one tower. From time to time I had tried to figure out why it seemed so familiar while it was only the first time I had seen it. If I could think hard enough, so it seemed to me, I should be able to figure out where I had seen it. And the image would dangle before me like a fish on the end of the rod, seemingly close enough to grab it yet frustratingly unreachable. I had never succeeded in solving the puzzle.

Frau Schuessler came in and poured the wine. "To whom shall we drink?" she said. "Oh, I know: to Fanny, that she may have a successful year of learning."

"To Fanny," said Leon and winking at me, then we clicked glasses and drank.

"Where is this place?" I asked and pointed at the painting.

"It's supposed to be an old fortress ruin in the north of France," she said. "It was a gift from a friend whose son had brought it back from France after the war. - So, let's see now; it's almost seven-thirty, the opera will start in a few minutes." She wore a pair of glasses that had only one half of a lens, the bottom part. My uncle Friedrich had used such glasses, and when he looked out over and above the lenses the impression was one of intense scrutiny. Frau Schuessler thumbed through the television guide, scrutinizing, and when she came to the right page, she read, "the barber is sung by Hermann Prey – great voice; and Rosina is sung by Erika Koeth - lovely coloratura soprano. Leon, have you been to the opera? How about you, Fanny?"

"We saw the operette the Fledermaus recently, does that count?" Leon asked.

"Not quite," said Frau Schuessler. "Although, The Barber of Seville is a comic opera, so it has a lot in common with an operetta."

"I saw Aida once on television, as a movie, with Sophia Loren in the title role."

"And the voices had been dubbed in; Sophia Loren is no singer. Muenchen has a great opera house and many great singers. You should take advantage of it," said Frau Schuessler. She quickly explained to us the story of the opera.

It was a new experience for me. I forgot the wine, the snacks that Frau Schuessler had brought in, I even forgot about Leon from time to time, except when he yawned. We were sitting very close, almost leaning on each other, but by the time the second act came around, Leon had fallen asleep. I nudged him a little, and when he came to, he earnestly rearranged his body in an upright position. I explained to him that count Almaviva wants to have a tete-a-tete with Rosina. Leon's valiant effort at staying upright caused his head to drop forward as he fell asleep again. Pretty soon he excused himself with regret. I walked him to the door to lock it after him. He apologized for his seeming lack of interest. He had had a very busy day and was just too tired.

It wasn't until December six, St. Nikolaus Day, which happened to be on a Saturday, that we managed to get together at his place. He had a small room in his brother Rudi's apartment above the butcher shop. Rudi and his wife had gone to play St. Nikolaus for the children of a friend.

Leon's room was sparsely furnished; there was a small wardrobe, a small table and matching chair, and a bed with a nightstand and small lamp. Above the bed hung a non-descript picture of what might have been a lovely landscape that had grown mostly gray with the years. There was also a small bookcase in the corner and on it lay the letters I had written to him after I had lost him the first time. It happened when Leon had left Hanfurt in the middle of our dance course, suddenly, and without a chance to let me know. After arriving in Muenchen he had written to me and explained his sudden departure. Mother had opened the letter and had never given it to me. But I had found it.

Leon sat down on the bed and pulled me down beside him. He took my hands into his and looked at me, his face expressed – I could not tell what. He seemed to have a hard time getting out what he wanted to say; finally, like giving himself a mental push, he said, "Fanny, dear sweet Fanny, I love you very much. Will you marry me?"

Oh, how I had wanted to hear that! How I had hoped for this gentle, loving man to be forever mine. I threw my arms around him and shouted, "oh, how I love you! Yes, yes, yes!" Leon grabbed me joyfully and hugged and kissed me wildly until I was quite out of breath.

When we had settled down we lay on his bed, side by side, and he caressed me as we talked about our future. He knew that I didn't like for him to kill animals. It didn't have to be that way, he said. He could work in the meat packing industry, or he could work as a meat inspector for the government. And my education? We are modern people, he said, a woman doesn't have to be stuck in the house. I should go ahead with my education, and if I didn't have time to cook then he would do it because he enjoyed cooking. We would have our own apartment, and in the mornings he would go to work and I would go to school.

"It's like a dream – just three months ago I was tormented by the fear that I might have lost you."

"Say yes, my love, say yes..." Leon sang in the words of the operetta.

"Do you remember the first time I asked you how many siblings you have?"

"I sure do; when I walked you home from our first dance lesson."

"That's right. And I was bragging of having so many siblings, but you have even more."

"Ten boys and just one girl."

"Wow! I wonder what that's like, especially for the one and only girl. She could be like a sister to me, and your brothers – forget the brother; I have enough brothers of my own," and I couldn't help laughing about the prospect of having ten more brothers. "But what about Christmas? You should come home with me and meet my family. And then I could meet your family, too."

"I don't think so, my love. Christmas is such an intimate family affair, you know? Besides, I want to start looking for our own place."

"Guess Hildi will have to wait a while longer."

"Your little sister knows about me?"

"Oh sure. She knows everything. I wouldn't be able to keep secrets from her if I wanted to. She's psychic." Leon looked at me with a blank expression. I could see that this topic had never been introduced to him.

"I'm going to cry on Christmas," I said.

"Why?"

"It's always so beautiful in the church during midnight mass. They turn off the lights, and then only the altar area and the two huge evergreen trees with millions of little white lights are lit, and then they play Silent Night, and it's all so beautiful that I cry, every time. And I don't even know why."

"Shouldn't you be happy?"

"That's right. And in a way, I am. But then the tears come anyway. And I wish that this beautiful moment would last forever, but it never does. Maybe that's why the tears come."

"You are a complicated sweetheart," Leon said and kissed me gently.

"What about your brother Rudi; have you told him about me?"

"Not yet. I'll tell him pretty soon. Anyhow, he will guess it when he sees a ring on my finger, which reminds me that we have to go shopping." and Leon hugged and kissed me again, and I felt so very happy that I began to wonder what life might have in store for us. Didn't religion teach us that life is a valley of tears!

I lay awake that night thinking about the midnight mass and what it could be that made me cry. Then I remembered other occasions that had brought out the same feelings. I remembered sitting at the edge of a meadow under a blue sky and warm sun, not a lawn but a meadow in its natural state. It was dotted with flowers, and graceful grasses wafted to and fro in a gentle breeze, and insects were buzzing lazily from one flower to the next. I sat and sat, taking in the utter contentment of that sight, wanting to be there always, but getting up and leaving with a most peculiar sense of restlessness. And the beautiful scenes of Western movies that I saw as a kid and could never get enough of, scenes of majestic landscapes and prairies and wide open spaces where I wished to be riding horseback with the wind in my face and nothing and nobody infringing on my freedom to run, to ride as far and as fast as I pleased. And very often, the movie soundtrack, that I could hear from our bathroom window, was so beautiful that I would hurry to listen to it every time the movie ran, which was exactly every two hours. And the music alone could stir me to tears. Why, I asked myself – why? But I could not get an answer.

Father's rent check for November finally arrived on December seven. He probably thought now that since he just sent out a check he was done for a while. I had to call home and remind him that it was now December, and sure enough, he thought he had already sent it. Then followed days of squabbling over which month had just gotten paid. Frau Schuessler's admonishment against such late and irregular payments caused me embarrassment every time I saw her. I wrote a letter to my mother, trying to make her understand my situation and asked her to take over the payment duty or let Hans do it. At seventeen he was certainly old enough to write out a check, have Father sign it, and mail it to me.

We bought a pair of wedding rings, simple gold bands without any decoration but with our names and date etched into the inside. After they had been sized we went to the little church and Leon put my ring on my left hand. As he slipped it on my finger he said with much solemnity, "I love you forever." Then I put his ring on his left hand, saying "I will always love you." Then we hugged and kissed, and I couldn't have cared less if anyone saw us. We sat quietly for a while, enjoyed the silence, held hands that exchanged unspoken messages of enduring love, and reveled in our own private little heaven.

When was the first time you thought about marrying me?"

"When I walked you home after our first dance lesson."

"Really?"

"Really," he said and looked at me with eyes so full of love that tears rose in my eyes.

School was out on December fifteen. I had earned good grades and felt very good about my success. On the next day I took the bus to Leon's butcher shop. I wanted to meet his brother without him knowing who I was. When I couldn't get anyone other than one of the sales girls to wait on me, and after I had picked out some sausage to take home, I asked if I could talk to Herr Rudi Kramer. The girl called through the door behind the counter, and the man who came out introduced himself as Rudi Kramer. He was a tall man, taller than Leon and thinner. I knew he was a little older than Leon, but not as old as he appeared with his gray complexion and deep furrows down the side of his nose and past the corners of his mouth. His eyes were deep set and had an expression of harshness about them. I asked him to tell me the meat content of the sausages I had just picked out. He looked puzzled at first, as though he wondered about the state of my mind, but then he told me. I thanked him, then he turned and went back to his domain of meat cutting and sausage making.

When I saw Leon that evening he told me that he had observed the whole thing through the window in the door, and how his brother had wondered about this customer who asked such dumb questions. Didn't everyone know what kind of meat a certain type of sausage is made of! It made me laugh.

"I'm going home Monday," I told him, "and I'm not looking forward to it. I'll miss you so much."

"I'll pick you up in Rudi's car and take you to the station. I don't often borrow it, so I'm sure he'll let me have it. He likes to hold his higher status over me, you know; he's the owner of his own shop, drives a Mercedes, his wife owns a fur coat. So, sometimes he gets under my skin and then we clash. I think getting out from under him will be good for me – and for you, my sweet wife because you'll have the happiest husband in the world! Let's get together Sunday evening. Rudi and his wife are going to some fancy event, a Christmas party, I think. We'll have the house to ourselves. Do you want to?"

"Oh yes! I've been hoping for some time alone with you."

When Leon came to pick me up he said, "today is the day." It sounded like a confirmation of an upcoming event, and there was something different in his demeanor as he gazed at me in silence for a long moment. Then he took me into his arms and held me, just held me a long time, not saying a word. How I loved these moments of closeness. Leon knew it. I couldn't remember Father ever holding me. Mother only hugged babies.

When I was ready to leave we took the next bus back to his place. I sensed something unusual going on in Leon; he hardly said a word, just sat beside me and held my right hand. My engagement ring gleamed in streetlights and bus lights. I turned my hand, moved it this way and that to catch the shine from this brand new, most precious piece of – no, not jewelry. I couldn't think of it that way. This ring was more precious than simple jewelry. It was a promise, a sign of commitment for the rest of our lives, something to show to the world that we two, Leon and I, belonged together.

It made me think of certain birds, the kind that pairs up for the rest of their lives. How they can find each other after having been apart for weeks and months, and while they look like a million other birds just like them, never ceased to amaze me. By their voices, science says, but it really doesn't explain anything. How can they even hear each other over millions of other voices, much less tell them apart. That surely was one of the miracles of nature.

"We're here," Leon said, pulling me out of my reflections. We got off the bus, then he took my arm into his, and we walked the few blocks to his home. The stores we came by were decorated for Christmas. I wished I could stay with Leon. I was not looking forward to seeing my parents, only the Christmas celebration. But Father would not allow it. Christmas was family time, and I was expected to be there. On the other hand, Christmas Eve was Mother's happy day, that one day of the year when she seemed truly happy, would sing blissfully off-key, and glow with pleasure because she had company. It would, therefore, be a happy day for us children as well. Leon was probably right by not coming with me. He would have been a disturbance to Father who would be forced to communicate with a stranger. He would want to know what kind of work Leon did; being a butcher, even a master butcher, was not Father's ideal for a son-in-law. And Mother, who did not like to be reminded of her own lowly heritage, would feel put upon by a guest who lacked every kind of distinguishing credential. Yes, it was better to wait till later.

It hadn't rained for a couple of days, so the sidewalks were dry. We reached the door to Leon's upstairs apartment very quickly. He unlocked the door, let me enter and then locked the door behind me. Then he took my hand and we climbed the long staircase to the second floor. He opened the apartment door, we went inside and into his room, and he locked the door behind us. He seemed tense, or anxious, or – I didn't know what to call his unusual disposition.

I looked around. On a table stood a bouquet of seven red roses beside a pretty dish with Christmas cookies, a couple of glasses and a bottle of champagne. We took off our coats. Leon pointed to the roses and said, looking into my eyes, "dunkelrote Rosen bring ich Dir, schoene Frau..." in the words of the operetta. I felt a little awkward at this compliment. I had never thought of myself as beautiful because religion called it being vain, and vanity was one of the seven deadly sins. But Leon said it, and Leon meant it, and I decided to accept his compliment without reservations. It made me smile with a kind of pleasure I had never experienced before.

I took the vase and buried my nose among the roses and sniffed them. Then I handed them back to Leon and said, "I should leave them with you since I'm leaving tomorrow. And I think I'll leave my ring with you, too. I can't let my father know that I'm engaged to be married since I just started school. He just might stop making payments. So, please, dear Leon, keep my ring till I get back. I will miss you terribly." I took the ring off and handed it to him. He laid it down carefully beside the roses.

Then he turned to face me, and his eyes looked at me with such passion that I felt weak in the stomach, and I knew what he would say. "I love you, Fanny. I love you more than anything in the world. I want you so much, I can hardly bear it." His face dropped on my shoulder, his hands held me tight, his body pressed into mine, and suddenly, the woman I had never known emerged and allowed Leon to undress her slowly, gently, kissing and caressing her body all the while until she lay down and opened herself for Leon to love.

Never in my life had I been as happy and carefree as in the embrace of Leon's love. Gone were the fear and anxiety that had been part of my daily life, the often unbearable tension and worry about punishment that had plagued me when I had followed my own inclination, which had always differed from that of my parents but especially Mother. And gone was the dreadful pain and loneliness I had suffered for years, when I couldn't be in a crowd of young couples who demonstrated with every moment what I was missing, without suffering an emotional breakdown. Now I understood what it meant to feel light as a cloud.

When I arrived in Hanfurt three days before Christmas, it was getting dark and drizzly outside. Hildi and the little boys had come to the station to meet me. The boys, Markus and Matthias, no longer so little, but much younger than Hans who was now seventeen and Walter who was twenty-two, danced around me like a couple of jumping beans. I snatched one after the other and kissed them soundly. Markus looked embarrassed and wiped away what I had planted on his face. I laughed. Then I turned to Hildi and hugged and kissed her. I must have been glowing with love because she stepped back a little, carefully examined me from head to toe while I closed my eyes and stood still like a model, knowing what she was doing. Her face broke out in a big happy smile then and she said, "You're happy." and she hugged me again as if she needed to express her own happiness at seeing me happy.

"How are things with - you know who?" I said to her as I took my suitcase and followed the boys down the street. Hildi was fourteen now, and I knew that she had a crush on Jordan from the sales department of Father's business.

"He went to work someplace else," she said without much emotion. Then she put her arm in mine.

"Tell me about it after we get these wild boys settled down, okay?" And the boys, hearing themselves called wild, decided to live up to that depiction and jumped around and jostled each other from the station all the way down the street to our home.

The store windows along the way glittered and gleamed in Christmas lights and décor and multiplied endlessly their reflections in the wet sidewalks, creating that special excitement which is particular to Christmas and had stayed with me since childhood. We had only two blocks to walk, but one or the other of the boys stopped at each one of the store windows to examine the beautiful wares. When we finally arrived at home Hans, with a book in his hand, opened the door and said with a broad grin, "what took you so long?" For a moment, I didn't know him. He had grown taller, and his face seemed more square. He had become a young man, taller than I and with a replica of Father's characteristic smile that made him look bashful. He gladly settled for a handshake. Then he went back to reading his book. And Hans had many books.

Hearing the commotion in the entry where we took off our coats, a young woman appeared from the kitchen. "You must be Fanny," she said and shook my hand. "The kids have been talking so much about you that I feel like I known you. I'm Helga, you probably heard of me?"

"Yes, Hildi mentioned you." Helga was Mother's new housemaid, a nice looking young woman, and probably only a few years older than I. She had an air of self-confidence and firmness about her that surely served her well with the little boys who were nine and eight years old now, and Mother who could see anything from only one perspective – her own. Helga went back to the kitchen, and I turned to Hildi and asked, "Mother is still downstairs?"

"Yes, don't worry."

"Okay then, come help me unpack. Do I still have a bed or has someone else got it now?"

"It's yours. I put fresh sheets on it because the boys sometimes sleep in it."

She opened my suitcase and began taking out my clothes. She loved to see my pretty things, something she hoped to own herself one day. Up to now she had never had anything better than hand-me-downs, if not from me then from our older sister Paula.

"How come you didn't bring Leon?"

"He thought since Christmas is such an intimate family affair that the presence of a stranger would be disturbing. You know how Dad is. But there's plenty of time to meet him."

Hildi stopped then and watched me. Suddenly she asked "are you getting married?"

"What? What makes you say that?"

"Oh Fanny, your aura! When I mentioned Leon, it turned brighter than I ever saw it."

Suddenly, an indescribable feeling of pain surged through me and tears welled up in my eyes. Hildi plopped down on her bed and looked at me as if she had seen a ghost. Moments later, without saying a word, she jumped up and ran from our room. I stopped what I was doing, just sat on the floor in front of my open suitcase and wept. I felt as though half of me had been torn away, and for the first time in my life I had a feeling of dread at the thought of being alone.

My tears kept flowing, I could not stop. Not until the little boys came running in was I able to gain some control. I had spent a lot of time with them after graduation from the boarding school. They knew me well, and seeing me wiping my eyes, Markus said, "Fanny, what's the matter?"

" I really don't know, little brother. Don't you worry, I'll be alright."

"You gotta know why you're crying," Markus insisted.

"You would think so, I know."

"Did you get us presents?" Matthias wanted to know.

"Oh, I'm sorry," I said. I didn't have money for gifts. I'm not working now, you know, just going to school."

"What do you learn in your school. What kind of school is it anyway?" Markus asked.

I explained to them why I, at the age of twenty, was still, or again, going to school. Then we talked about their plans for the future, as I had done in the past so as to get their thinking and planning going in the right direction. I didn't want them to end up like me, just waiting to be told what to do, when, and how to do it. Father was more generous with the boys, though; he actually had plans for Hans to become a military officer – like Father's older brother, John, whom he had admired, who had died in WWI and lay buried somewhere in France. Perhaps Father had realized by now that lying dead in a foreign land didn't do anybody any good. Perhaps he had even discovered that Hans hadn't the least little interest in such a career. But I doubted it.

The matter of Walter and his future had been easily solved since he was the crown prince of family and business assets. Of course he could have been contrary by wanting to become a hairdresser, or shoe salesman, or a priest. But Walter had agreed to take over the family business. He had completed an apprenticeship and had started work in the family business around the same time I had left for Muenchen.

Shortly after six o'clock Mother and Father came upstairs from the store on the street level. Mother loved being in the store, being admired by customers for having so many children, a huge garden, and working in the store as well. Father, when he saw me, broke out in his singular smile – the corners of his mouth went down instead of up, and it made him appear bashful, or embarrassed. He shook my hand, and asked after Frau Schuessler's well-being. Mother had lost control over me and no longer seemed to care much about what I was doing. She shook my hand, put on her company smile, and gave me a look of disapproval when she noticed my slacks. I pretended not to notice.

Helga had prepared a cold supper for the children who were eating in the dining room. "Aren't you hungry?" she said to me when she saw me walking aimlessly down the long corridor that connects the apartment door on one end to the large dining room that was a later addition to the house on the other end. Bathroom, kitchen and playroom were located on one side of the corridor and faced the loading yard of Father's business. My parents' bedroom, the living room, and three more bedrooms that were not directly accessible from the corridor were located on the side that faced the street.

"Sure I'm hungry," I replied and couldn't help smile as I remembered Father's efforts at directing traffic in this long corridor: You walk on the right and pass on the left, he had taught us. He had also taught us how to watch for traffic. You look to your right, then to your left, and then to the right again before crossing the street. And you never ever cross an intersection. And since we knew that he could and would observe us from our third floor apartment windows we behaved and did as we were told.

I went to the dining room and sat with the kids to eat a cold supper of sandwiches and milk. Father and Mother would get their meals served in the living room.

"Where's Walter?" I asked.

"He's out with his buddies. They probably drink a lot. Then he stays out till all hours," Hans said with disdain.

"And they play cards," Matthias chimed in.

"You're never going to do that, are you" said Markus. I looked at Hans, he had a sheepish grin on his face, but he answered, "no, never."

"Hah!" voiced Hildi. But she said no more. She busied herself with her food, saw to it that the little guys didn't cut the crust from their bread because they didn't want to eat it, and reprimanded them when their eating manners were not up to par. But she never looked at me.

I didn't dare think about that dreadful feeling to avoid crying again. I was just glad that I had company. And Hildi's puzzling behavior of running out of the room gave me a lot to think about. She had always been affectionate with me, had confided in me and was sad for me when I had lost Leon the first time. And Hildi had been happy for me when I found Leon again. But now she seemed to shy away from me. Perhaps it was for the best since I had always felt bad for leaving Hildi, whose learning problems had caused Mother to lose patience and slap her. We ate in silence, only the boys jabbered on the way they always did. They were only one year apart and very much alike in their appearance. Markus, the older one, tended to be introspective, but Matthias, the youngest, had learned early on to defend himself with flippancy and even a little aggressiveness against so many older siblings.

After I had read them a story that night and they had gone to bed, I sat with my parents and watched television. There was nothing else to do. Mother wanted to know why I hadn't come home earlier, since my school had let out several days ago. I told her that I liked it in Muenchen, and had used my free time to explore the city.

"You should have come home right away. There's work to be done. Helga is going home tomorrow, so you and Hildi will have plenty to do. The tree will be delivered tomorrow, and you can decorate it in the dining room…" And Mother went on and on as if I had never left home. It was as if she still saw me as under her control, existing for the sole purpose of doing her bidding.

It was just like those times when I had come home from boarding school. She had shown no interest in me and my life, as if I had none, or whatever life I had only existed in relation to what I could do for the family. At fifteen, coming home on vacation, this utter indifference had brought on a crisis that had made me take the next train back to boarding school. I had been happy there. Father had realized then that I needed more attention, but Mother had never changed.

Good God! What would I do without Leon, it suddenly hit me and a sting of pain went through me. I resolved to leave right after Christmas Day and not stay for Epiphany on January six. Next morning I went to the railroad station to check out train schedules for December twenty-nine. Then I sent a letter to Leon and let him know on which train I would return, and asked him to meet me at the station.

Hildi and I set up and decorated the Christmas tree and the nativity, then Mother locked the door to that room. There was shopping to be done, and baking, and cleaning, and buying the ingredients for our Christmas goose dinner. On the afternoon of Christmas Eve Father took us to the cemetery where we visited his parents and two brothers. It was one of Father's traditions and the only time we learned a tiny bit about the previous generation. In the family plot lay his parents, his brother Ernst who had died of an illness at age fifteen, and the name of his brother John, buried somewhere in France, was chiseled into the headstone. Nearby was the grave of a maiden aunt, a sister to Father's mother. And in the old part of the cemetery lay his baby brother and sister. This visit to the cemetery was like the final duty before the giddy fun part of opening presents on Christmas Eve.

And when it was time, Mother came for us with her blissful smile. She and Father led us to the Christmas tree that glittered in the light of real candles, which were reflected thousand fold in heavy tinsel and shiny ornaments. It was a glorious sight to behold. We sang carols, and the little boys recited Christmas poems by the nativity. Our presents were, as always, spread out on table, chairs, and sideboard, for each one of us our own little pile. We didn't know which pile belonged to whom until Mother took us by the hand and led us to it. There was a guitar for Hans, and a mandolin for Hildi. Walter received a ring of gold with the family crest emblazoned on it. Markus and Matthias got some new toys, I received useful items for a dowry. And there were the usual useful items like pajamas, and house slippers, hankies, socks, and perfumed soap.

Father became frisky then. He sang the song about the Christmas tree with many lights, and Walter eagerly joined him, but he changed the words and sang about a prune that his dumb brother had hung on the tree. We knew he was singing about the brother with whom Father managed the family business but could never get along. The words rhymed so well that it made us laugh, and Mother scolded with mock indignation, "Husband! Stop that!"

Everyone went to Midnight Mass, even the little boys wanted to go. Staying up way past bedtime gave them that much desired illusion of being grown up. The altar of my parish church, built in early baroque style, was loaded with flowers, and dozens and dozens of candles were burning. Even the side altars were decorated with flowers and candles. To the right and left of the main altar stood the two evergreen trees that I had mentioned to Leon. They were covered in a multitude of little white electric lights that appeared as stars. As always, at the end of mass all the lights were turned off, and only the altar area with the twinkling Christmas trees was lit. In anticipation of the most beautiful of Christmas songs my eyes began to fill with tears, and soon the tears ran down my face while we sang Silent Night, Holy Night. And while the beauty of the night held sway I turned inward and discovered that my tears were caused by the pain of knowing that all earthly beauty will fade away. Ever so hesitantly, I carried this thought a little further and wondered if 'all earthly beauty' included the love that Leon and I had for each other.

Paula and Werner came for Christmas dinner and brought along the twins who where now eighteen months old. I had been their Nanny in the time before I started school in Muenchen. Werner's lascivious look at me had not changed. I shook hands, no more. Paula looked tired. Tired of the twins or tired of Werner - only she could know. Father had always enjoyed babies, and he missed no opportunity to show his delight with the twins. While Father knew how to have fun with them, Mother leaned more toward proper discipline, and she was quick to correct Paula in her dealings with the twins. Paula and I didn't talk much; since I didn't share with anyone my life with Leon, there wasn't much to say. The same seemed to be true for her, except that in her case reluctance to talk surely had to do with her jerk of a husband. My parents had thought him to be a great catch because Werner had a profession and owned his own shop. With this conviction uppermost in their minds, it had never occurred to them that Werner was human like everyone else, perhaps even more so. But Werner was good company for Walter who had no company in Father because Father was forty years older. Other than business, they had nothing in common and literally lived on different strata. That's where Werner's presence did some good, for he presented a kind of middle ground.

Playing with the twins was for me a welcome distraction from the tears that were a constant threat. And Walter's humor and jokes and one-liners and wittily corrupted lines of well-known classical poetry were hilarious. I was grateful for the change in mood. Only Erna, my oldest sister, was not with us. She had died in a car accident three years earlier.

I was restless the following day, the twenty-sixth; it was also kept as a religious and state holiday. Mother did not have to work in the store but instead, worked in the kitchen. I had to help her with cooking which I didn't mind, but being in her presence always made me feel uneasy. Hildi continued to stay out of my way, so after dinner I went for walks in the old familiar places where Leon and I had been. Snow, which tends to add romance to the holiday, did not materialize. But at least there was no rain. By late afternoon I took the boys to various churches to view the nativity scenes that each one had set up. The churches were open for that purpose, the lights were on, and everywhere lots of real live evergreen trees were part of the nativity backgrounds and exuded the wonderful fragrances of firs and spruces. Hildi did not want to come along.

I woke up more at ease on the twenty-eighth. This was the day I would see Leon again. My insides did flip-flops at the thought of it. I went to Father's office on the second floor – our apartment was on the third floor of the family house. I told Father what my plan was and that I needed the money to get back to Muenchen. He wanted to know why I didn't stay till Epiphany. I came up with some excuse, but Father never accepted anything that didn't agree with his mindset. He expected me to stay with the family during this family time. I was beginning to feel that awful tension again, the tension that tied up my insides, that arose from having my plans and wishes run roughshod over. Is Walter staying till then, I asked, knowing full well that he had gone skiing with friends. Father said no more. We talked a while longer; he seemed more receptive in his office than in the apartment. I brought up the late and irregular payments and that they embarrassed me. I suggested that Hans could remind him on the first of each month, make out the check and then mail it to me. Father agreed. Then he gave me a check for my support during the next quarter. I went to the bank to cash it.

I said good-bye to Mother with a handshake. Then I went downstairs to say good-bye to Father. The boys were disappointed that I was leaving so soon, but since Helga was an effective buffer between them and Mother, I had no qualms about leaving them. The boys took me to the station, but Hildi pretended to have something important to do and could not come. Then, at the front door, I turned to Hildi; her eyes avoided mine. To my question what was wrong, she denied that anything was. Then she quickly hugged me, turned and went back to her room. I already felt bad about the seeming split in our relationship, and this behavior made me feel worse. What had I done to her, I wondered.

The boys had gone ahead to the station with my suitcase. I reached them at the platform on which my train would be leaving.

"The train will stop for only one minute, so you have to hurry," said Hans.

"And you remind Dad that you are going to write out the checks from now on and mail them to me on the first of the month, right?"

"Right."

"Okay you little monsters, give me a hug and a kiss."

"I'm getting too big for that," said Markus. So I shook hands with him and Hans, but Matthias grabbed me around the neck, hard, and planted a fat kiss on my cheek. The fast Intercity train from Hamburg pulled in; it would stop for only one minute. I got onboard, turned around, waved to the boys, and the train took off.

Time on the train to Muenchen passed too slowly. My excitement over seeing Leon again stirred up my insides and made me nearly sick with happy anticipation. I could not concentrate on anything, could not doze, could not read. Finally around four-thirty the train arrived in the main railroad terminal. For a moment I feared that I might have forgotten to tell Leon at which station I would arrive. But a train from Hamburg could only arrive at the main station. Leon, surely, knew this.

I could hardly wait for the train to come to a complete stop; I stood on the top step and took a quick look around for Leon. I couldn't see him anywhere. Perhaps too many people are blocking my view, I thought and waited till everyone had left the platform. But Leon was not there. I walked toward the area beyond the tracks where kiosks and ads and fast-food stands were lit up on this dark afternoon. I looked and waited, and looked and waited. Perhaps he had to hurry to a bathroom; perhaps he never got my letter; perhaps his watch had stopped. I kept thinking of excuses, but finally I had to admit that Leon simply had not come. I was shaking from disappointment and the drafty cold of the station platform on which not only trains pulled in but cold winds as well. What could have happened? Maybe he couldn't get his brother's car. Then he would have taken a cab, I was sure of it.

Before the turmoil in my insides got any worse I had to find out. I took a cab and went to Leon's home. It was just minutes after six o'clock when I arrived, and the shop was closed. I rang the bell to the upstairs apartment and waited. Someone looked out from an upstairs window, and I asked, "is Leon home?"

The answer was "no."

"I need to talk to Leon," I called out.

"He is not here. Who are you?"

"I'm Stephanie." The person at the upstairs window seemed to think for a moment then closed the window and came downstairs. Fear began to grip me; fear that I would not find Leon. Rudi opened the door.

"Where is Leon?"

"Come on in, Stephanie" he said in a soft voice. He locked the door behind me. "Let's go upstairs."

"Where is Leon?" I shouted in desperation. Rudi turned around and looked at me. Despite the dim light of the stairway I could see that his face had a somber expression. My legs began to give out; leaning against the wall I began to slide down to the floor, crying, "where is he?"

Rudi turned back and helped me up the stairs. He led me to the living room and to a sofa where he sat down beside me. "Stephanie, listen," he said softly while looking at me and holding my hands. "Leon died. He died in a motorcycle accident."

My mind twisted his words into unrecognizable sounds. "What?"

"Leon died in a motorcycle accident."

I remember hearing a long drawn out, hysterical "nooo," then I must have passed out.

When I came to I was lying on Leon's bed, and Rudi and his wife were bending over me. Then I remembered what Rudi had said to me – that Leon had died. And suddenly, I understood that intense feeling of pain that had come over me when I was unpacking my suitcase, the feeling that half of me had been torn away. And indeed, it had.

"It happened around five o'clock in the afternoon on the twenty-first, didn't it," I said in a tone that lacked all emotion.

"How did you know that?" Rudi asked, astonished.

"And I couldn't even be at the funeral." And then the tears came, and the pain overwhelmed me. Rudi and his wife decided to give me some privacy. If I needed anything I was to call.

I lay on the bed where Leon and I had made love, and I cried in agony. My body ached with yearning for his embrace. I wanted to lose myself in the recollection of that blissful night. But Leon was gone, and I would never see him again. Never again would his arms hold me, never again would he make love to me. I wept until exhaustion overtook me and I fell asleep.

I woke up sometime during the night but went back to sleep until a knock at the door woke me up. It was Maria, Rudi's wife. She asked me if I wanted some breakfast. She stood in the open door but seemed reluctant to come in. There was something about her that I didn't like. I thought it best to leave. I told her I only wanted to use the bathroom.

"I think you know where it is," she said and looked at me like…." I didn't have the strength to figure it out. I didn't care what she thought. I just wanted to get away. I opened my suitcase, fished out my toiletries and went to the bathroom. I threw some cold water in my face, combed my hair and straightened out my clothes. Then I remembered my engagement ring, and I asked Maria to give it to me. I had not seen it in Leon's room. Maria claimed not to have seen it.

"I left it on the table for Leon to keep till I got back. He told you that we were engaged to be married, didn't he?"

"No."

"Didn't you see a ring on his finger when you buried him?"

"No, I didn't."

"Leon and I were engaged to be married and he bought two rings. He wore one and I wore the other, and our names are engraved in them. Please, I need it, it's the only thing I have of him."

"I'll ask Rudi if he has seen it," she said. "He's busy in the shop now." I didn't believe her, but decided to take it up with Rudi at a later date.

I left the apartment, went downstairs and waited for the Taxi that Maria had ordered for me. I could have cried again at the thought that our precious love nest, the most blissful place I had ever known, to be occupied by a woman who, it seemed to me, didn't care much for Leon.

The cab came and took me to Frau Schuessler's house. I went directly to my room, threw myself on the bed and wept again. When I had no more tears left, I lay on my back and stared into nothing. Stared at the ceiling, the walls, the door, the window. Finally, hunger made me get up and go to the kitchen for something to eat. Frau Schuessler was not at home. I hadn't told her when to expect me back. Then I took a bath. Soaking in the tub, I thought about that moment when sudden emotional pain had surged through me – it must have been at the moment when Leon died. His soul was freed from his body then, and it could connect with my soul. And my soul's knowledge of Leon's death transferred to my body and caused the emotional pain. Could it be like that, I wondered. I had to find out.

I got dressed and went to the living room. A note from Frau Schuessler lay on the table; she had gone to visit a friend over Christmas and New Year and would be back on the third of January. I sat down on the settee; my senses were straining to perceive something – anything. There was total silence, not even the tick-tock of a clock. I sat and sat, seeing myself alone and forgotten. Nobody knew where I was. Nobody knew of my pain and sorrow. It's as if I didn't exist – rather like the sound of the fallen tree in the forest that only exists if someone hears it. I had experienced the joy of becoming one with the object of my love. And now, loss of the bliss I had known broke my heart.

What do I do now, I wondered. I knew no one in Muenchen, had no place to go, no job to do, no purpose, no responsibility. School wouldn't start for ten days. I felt lost and forlorn, like a little heap of nothing within the endless universe. And my tears flowed again from pity for myself.

By mid-afternoon I had come to the decision to visit my girl friend Steffi in Wiesenthal. I called her to ask if it was alright for me to come. She was surprised to hear from me; I had neglected her since Leon had entered my life again. Tears prevented me from saying much about Leon. "Never mind," she said. "Just come. You can tell me all about it when you get here. And yes, it'll be okay with my parents, you know that, right?"

"Yes. See you tomorrow!"

Around six o'clock I went to the butcher shop to see Rudi about my ring. He invited me in and we talked about the accident. Leon's bike had slipped on the wet, mushy street and skidded under an oncoming truck. I started to cry again. What a horrible moment it must have been for Leon to know what was about to happen to him. Rudi knew that Leon and I were engaged, but he didn't know what had become of my ring. He had taken Leon's ring and had placed it beside mine on the little table in Leon's room. His mother and several of his brothers had come for the funeral, and he remembered his mother commenting on the rings, that Leon was engaged, and who the girl might be. Rudi couldn't tell her anything about me, except my name and that I was here in Muenchen. Perhaps she took the rings with her, I wondered. Perhaps, Rudi said.

The sun was shining when I arrived in Wiesenthal, and between sunshine and seeing Steffi again my mourning spirit began to improve a little. I walked to Steffi's house; I had done it twice before and knew the way. When I rang the downstairs bell she yanked open the window of her room on the second floor as if she had been standing there, just waiting for my ring. "Fanny!" she yelled, shut the window again and came racing downstairs to open the outside door. I had to smile; that was Steffi, skittish little Steffi from boarding school days – now all grown up.

She came flying out the door and hugged me, and I hugged her, and we went upstairs together, talking all at the same time. Once we entered her room, she looked at me with sad eyes and said, "I'm so very sorry about Leon. Tell me what happened."

Steffi had met Leon after I had found him again the first time. She knew him well enough to understand what I was missing. Tears were rising in my eyes again, but I forced them down. Then I told her about my last three months in Muenchen, how I had looked for and found Leon again, that I now had my own four walls and was going to school. It came poring out of me like a faucet turned to high.

"There is something I want to do," I told Steffi. "I want to talk with Judith while I'm here. I want to ask her if it's possible for me, or my body, or spirit – I just don't know exactly how to put it – for me to know the moment that he died. And – oh! I just had a thought. When that pain suddenly hit me, Hildi looked at me as if she had seen a ghost. She had asked me if I was getting married. My aura made her think so. I bet my pain was reflected in my aura too. What do you think?"

"I'm sure it was," said Steffi and nodded very seriously.

"And she didn't want to tell me, that's why she kept away from me."

"She sounds like a sweet kid."

"She is. Sensitive and loyal and caring. Amazing person, really. - Are you exercising your ESP any?"

"No, I don't. I'm busy with my music studies and endless violin practice. Besides, I figure it's more important for me to learn about people by observing them instead of their auras. Besides, you remember what happened to your sister Erna because I had a vision and thought I should keep her from getting killed in an accident!"

"And then she died anyway and you and I got the blame for making her so angry that she ran out of the house and right into a car."

"That still haunts me at times."

"I finally stopped feeling guilty," I said. "Feeling guilty was partly to blame for my submissiveness to Mother."

We talked for a long time about boarding school, which still made us laugh, about the summer she spent at my house with its convoluted teenage escape routes, about the time I had lived with her while going to work for a gynecologist. I hadn't written much because my relationship with Mother had been an ongoing battle of more or less intensity – utterly depressing.

"I better let Mom know that you're staying for dinner."

"Can I help you with anything?"

"No, you just stay put. But if you want to, you could go and see Judith right now. Maybe you don't even need an appointment."

"Yeah, that's an idea. I hope she's open." I freshened up a bit, put on my coat and headed for Judith whose little shop seemed to have no front door. I had to laugh at the way we had riddled about it the first time Steffi and I had gone to see her. Judith was a slightly chubby lady in her fortys, had long dark hair and wore a flowing gown that reached to the floor. And she had that same slightly mischievous grin on her face, a grin that seemed to say that she knew it all, had seen it all, and nothing could surprise her. She remembered me.

"You're in luck; I have time," she said. "Readings are very popular between the years, but I'm free right now. So, have a seat and then tell me what I can do for you."

I told her my sad story, and the tears came again. "What do you think?" I asked when I had finished.

"I'm so sorry for your unhappiness, but I think you got it right. In those last moments before he died, when he knew he was about to suffer a terrible accident, his last thoughts were of you. His consciousness – life and consciousness are two sides of the same coin, you know - his consciousness shifted to you and connected with yours. And that knowledge, received on the level of the higher mind, transferred down to the astral plane where it caused emotional pain, and then transferred to your physical body where it caused even physical pain. And yes, of course, your little sister Hildi could see that in your aura."

I was so pleased to hear that from Judith. "Do you think Leon is still around?"

"Sometimes, when death is sudden, the soul doesn't understand what happened to it and thinks it's still alive. But your Leon knows what happened to him, and your love is still so young and strong that it keeps him near you. Yes, he's around," she said with a smile as she looked toward my right side.

"Is he here?" I asked.

"Yes, he is; and if you close your eyes and concentrate real hard, you'll know it too."

"Just like that?"

"There are three things required to accomplish what you want: will, wisdom, and action. Will is the power that drives your purpose forward; wisdom is knowing the right way to go, the right path for you, and action is that which brings your effort to fruition. It takes practice, for sure, but so does everything new you'd want to learn."

We talked a while longer about how a spirit, while being on a higher level of existence than the living, can nonetheless be perceived by a loved-one on the physical level.

The way back to Steffi's house led across a little square that was bordered on one side by a high stonewall that supported a fountain and a stone bench on either side of it. Overhanging branches from a tall elm tree behind the wall made it a picturesque setting that Leon and I had enjoyed together when he had come from Muenchen to visit me during my long stay with the Rheins.

It had grown dark, and I wanted some time to myself before getting back to Steffi's house. Few people were out and about, so I sat down on the bench that Leon and I had used. I closed my eyes and built an image of Leon in my mind. And after a little while I began to feel that, indeed, I saw him looking at me with his gray eyes and beautifully kind and gentle smile. The tears came again, ran down my face and made it itch. It broke my concentration.

When I got back to Steffi's place, Frau Rhein had come upstairs from her husband's photography shop that was located on the street level. Steffi had filled her in about what had happened to Leon, and she was truly sad for me. And, yes, I was to stay a few days because it wasn't right that I should be alone over Sylvester, the last day of the year. After Herr Rhein came upstairs we sat down to a cold supper, and the talk led to some of the things people do to celebrate the incoming New Year. Steffi had been invited to a party at the house of her girl friend whose American GI would be there also. "I always have a good time there – lots of laughs. Her father can be very funny, but they drink a lot, and one time, they wouldn't let me go home, not until three o'clock in the morning." I must have looked doubtful, because she continued, "really! They actually locked the door, so I couldn't leave. But I don't really feel like going there tonight unless you want to come along?"

"No, I don't feel like it. But you can go; I don't mind."

"No, I don't want to go either. I can drink and laugh at her house any time. Let's watch TV. There's always a nice program on Sylvester."

I stayed with the Rheins till January six, Epiphany, then I went back to Muenchen. Frau Schuessler had returned, school started again, and so did life without Leon. The first few days kept me occupied with new subjects and materials, but once everything had settled down into a regular routine I began to feel the emptiness in my life. I had chosen Muenchen because Leon was there. But Leon was gone, and Muenchen was nothing to me. And now I was stuck here for the next five years. Alone. My classmates were younger than I and we had nothing in common other than the subjects we studied. I didn't care for a career anymore. I drudged along without interest or satisfaction. To escape the loneliness I went to bed and slept.

The January check to Frau Schuessler arrived on time. Once February rolled around it was the same old story, and Frau Schuessler became upset about the unreliability of her extra income. I knew that no matter what I would say or do, it would happen again. Crisis management was my parents' style of action, and nothing would change it.

I began to think about quitting school. But where would I go. I would lie on my bed for hours thinking about Leon, imagining him by my side, feeling his touch, seeing his sweet smile. Then I'd wake up to the here and now and cry my eyes out. My grades suffered, my teachers expressed concern but it didn't matter to me. Some mornings I didn't feel like getting up, missed classes because I didn't feel well. Miss Geisel tried to coax me into revealing what troubled me, but I didn't tell. I could not believe that she really, truly cared about me. I had never experienced real caring such as Leon was capable of. So I kept quiet and suffered.

In early March I received a note from the academy's administration warning me that if my grades didn't improve they would not admit me to the spring quarter. It was just as well, I thought. There was no way that I would spend five more years alone in Muenchen. There was nothing else to do but go home and hope for the best. I would find a job in Hanfurt; that would keep me out of the house for most of the day. And Walter, surely, went out a lot in the evenings. I couldn't see him staying home at night even just one day. What was there for him to do? Watching TV with my parents? Hardly. And when he went out, I would go with him.

When the quarter was over I packed my bags and left.

I took a very early train and hadn't told anyone that I was coming. The kids were in school, Father was in his office, and Mother was in the store waiting on customers when I arrived. I didn't even ring the doorbell but just let myself into the apartment and dropped off my luggage. Then I went to see Dr. Bloom, a lady doctor whom Mother had called whenever one of us children had been sick. She was a slender, middle age woman who wore a stylish hairdo and make-up. She remembered me from the time when I had had the mumps. She was friendly and asked me what kind of problems I might be having. In her office stood a table with stirrups, a frightful looking thing, like a torture instrument that made me shudder whenever I saw it. And I had always been relieved whenever I was allowed to pass it. But today I was not so lucky. After asking me a lot of questions, among them the date of my last period, Dr. Bloom had me lie on that dreadful thing in the most embarrassing position and examined me inside and out.

After I was dressed again, sitting in a chair that faced her desk while she sat behind it like a schoolmaster, she said that I had been pregnant. She looked at me with a searching eye, sitting quietly, watching for my reaction.

"What?"

"Did you have a very heavy period recently?"

"Yes. Huge blobs came out, and there was so much blood that I didn't dare go anywhere."

"You had a miscarriage."

" A miscarriage?"

"Yes. It's not unusual and nothing to worry about. And your uterus is clear, no dead tissue is left behind. That's good."

"Oh my God, I was pregnant!"

I didn't go home then. I went to the park, to the old linden tree that is surrounded by a bench. It had been witness to one of my emotional breakdowns when I had lost Leon the first time. I felt so bad about having lost a baby of which I had known nothing. And since it was the essence of Leon, the loss was doubly sorrowful. I closed my eyes and pictured myself telling Leon that we had a baby but lost it. The tears came again, ran down my face and made it itch. It broke my concentration.

When I returned home, the kids had come home from school. As always, they were happy to see me. Hildi looked at me with a sad expression, hugged me, and said she was so sorry.

"You knew that Leon died, didn't you," I said to her. She nodded, and tears came into our eyes. "And you didn't want to tell me, that's why you kept away?" She nodded. "What else did you see in my aura? By the way, you were right: we were engaged to be married."

"I saw your pretty colors become very dark, very suddenly. You felt real pain, didn't you."

"Yes, I did. It was awful. I felt as if half of me, half of my person, had been torn away. And then I found out that he really died just at the time when I felt that pain.

Hildi and I hugged and held on for a while until we both felt better. She was almost as tall as I now, going on sixteen; no longer the little girl who had trouble with her homework because she couldn't tell where to place a comma, or mixed up the letters of a word, or refused to use her right hand because the left hand was easier.

"What happened to him?" she asked. We sat down together and I told her the whole sad story. "I'm so sorry," she said again.

"And I didn't wear my ring because I didn't want Father to find out so he wouldn't make me quit school. But now, I don't care about a career anymore. And I don't want to live in Muenchen alone. That's why I came home. Keep it to yourself, though. Let them think for a while that I'm on break."

Hildi nodded and went to do homework, and the three boys did as well. I felt quite out of place, and very much alone. It's as if I no longer had a connection to my family, the kind that ties members together through common experiences and lasts a life time, even if one should move as far away as the South Pole. I had been away at boarding school for three years and Paula did not share in that experience. On my return Paula was engaged to be married, and I could not share in hers. Walter, as a boy, had led a life that was separate from us girls, and the same was true for Hans. And Hildegard, although a girl, was so much younger than I that she could not share to the same level in any of my experiences. Some day the little boys would be grown up, and the family stories that any of us knew would be mostly unknown to them.

I went out again, to my parish church that was always open during the day, to think about my future. First of all I had to find a job. The employment office was closed now; I would go there first thing in the morning. Meanwhile, I decided to pay Ulla a visit. I hadn't seen her since I left for Muenchen in

September. She was working in her father's stationary shop; it hadn't closed for the day yet, so I went inside. She looked surprised, pleasantly surprised; it made me feel good to see that someone was pleased to see me. When she had completed her transaction with the customer she came to me and we hugged and laughed and talked all at once. I made a date with her for the following day, late afternoon. We would meet at our favorite Café. Then I went home.

Father and Mother had come upstairs and were sitting in the living room watching the news. I went in to make my appearance – my report as Father would call it. Not much was said. Father, as always, asked after Frau Schuessler's well-being, Mother looked at me probingly – she never asked me anything about myself. The quarter was over, I was on break, I said, and nothing more transpired.

Early next morning I went to the employment office. Since I had education in business subjects and had worked in the office of a gynecologist for several months I was confident. And, indeed, an office job was available in the office of the export department of a local factory. The factory was growing, I learned; a new building had been built near the old one, and there, in a brand new office I was to work for the advertisement manager, taking dictation and typing letters. I was thrilled at my success. Father would not say much about dropping school in the light of gaining a job. I would start work on the following Monday.

Back home, I decided to take the empty room in the fourth floor attic for myself. Helga, our maid, didn't need the room because she went home at night. After noon-time dinner, Hans and Hildi helped me carry my stuff upstairs, the little boys had to be in on the move and brought my slippers and shoes. Then they helped me put sheets on the bed and find the toilet bucket, should I need to get up during the night. The boys thought it weird that I would actually pee into that bucket. "Well, what would you do, if you slept in this room and had to pee during the night? Would you go out into that dark hallway, and down that dark stairway and ring the bell to wake mom or dad to let you in and use the toilet?"

"No way!" shouted Matthias and Markus as with one voice, but they tried it out just for fun anyway. They sat down on the bucket to see how it would fit their butts. They figured they would probably fall in, and they laughed and teased each other. In the storage room next to the bedroom I found the old gramophone and it still worked. And even my favorite record still existed, though way too scratched to be played anymore. I had not only listened to that record, I had used it to save my sanity, although unaware of it at the time. Whenever the pain of loneliness had become unbearable I had played this record; its poignant tune had always moved me to tears, and the tears had brought relief. But why should I have had so much emotional pain! It could not have been part of the teenage experience because other girls, like Ulla and Steffi, were not like that. And a couple of others I knew from elementary school, and whom I had met again at the German-American Friendship Club when Ulla and I had gone dancing there, they were not lonely. Why had I been in so much pain before I knew Leon? Because I missed being loved? But how could I miss something I had never experienced? Who had ever shown me love? Who had ever shown me affection, or held me close to make me feel protected? There had only been punishment and rebuke.

Next day I went to meet Margarete, Leon's only sister, who worked at the downtown branch of the savings bank. When I entered the bank building I felt again, as I had often done, an atmosphere of cold, impersonal, punitive authority. It was the very opposite of entering a church. I asked for Margaret Kramer, and to the question of who wants her I replied, Stephanie. After a short wait a door opened and she came toward me. She was a somber looking young woman, older than Leon, short of stature and not very pretty, and she was dressed in black. She introduced herself, then she motioned me to come to her office. After she had closed the door we turned to each other, and thinking that I was looking at Leon's sister, a person who had spent more time with him than I would ever have, the pain it caused me brought out the tears again.

"I know who you are," she said with a smile; you're Leon's betrothed, aren't you." I nodded. "Come, sit down," she said, then pulled up another chair and sat down beside me. Then we talked a little. She didn't have much time for me since she was on the job. Before I left, she wrote down her mother's address on a piece of paper and gave it to me. To my question if her mother would want to see me, she replied, "most definitely. You couldn't do her any greater favor than to talk with her about Leon."

"May I give you a hug?" I asked. Instead of an answer she put her arms around me and hugged me, and kissed me on the cheek. Then she smiled at me and said, "go, see Mother. You'll be glad you did."

Saturday evening brought a favorite television program; it was a play, a comedy with a famous comic actor by the name of Heinz Erhardt in the title role. The kids were watching along with us. "How long will you be staying," Mother asked during the play. I thought it a good time to say what I had to say while her attention was elsewhere.

"I'm not going back to Muenchen. Monday I'm starting a job at the felt factory," I said, watching myself remain calm and without fear. Just then there was loud laughter, then it was quiet.

"What did you say?" Mother asked, her face turned to the television.

"I'm not going back to Muenchen, I'm starting a job on Monday here in Hanfurt."

Father and Mother looked at each other for a moment, then they looked at me, but they said nothing because the play was just too funny and neither wanted to miss any of it.

But they did say something about it the following day. Once again, I stood before them like a poor sinner, my eyes focused on the carpet to study its pattern while Father paced up and down, ranting about the money I had thrown away, his

54

money, by starting something and not finishing it. Mother pointed out that, once again, I had run away from something, that I could not be trusted to make the right decision and would have to be told what to do. Neither of them asked for the reasons why. And I knew that I would have a fight on my hands again, a fight to keep me out from under Mother's thumb.

Finally I realized that I was still playing the guilty part, standing there in quiet submission while the lord and lady heaped shame on me. I looked up and said, "I don't want to hear any more." Then I turned and walked out.

"You come back here!" Mother called after me. I didn't care.

This utter indifference to me and the reasons for my actions, which otherwise might have produced understanding and compassion, made me as miserable as I had always been at home. But it was much worse now. Since Leon had entered my life I had known real love, had begun to feel and desire and to believe in a happy future. And now, having lost Leon and his love, life in an environment of utter indifference would be worse than ever.

I waited up for Walter that evening, and when he came home, very late, I asked him to drive me to Rhoenhausen on Sunday so I could visit Leon's mother. It wasn't easy to get him to agree. Like Father, Walter was not used to thinking of the rest of us, never asked to do something for us girls or the little kids. Mother had never placed duties on the heir apparent, so nothing was ever required of him within the family. I confided in him my sad story, that I had been engaged to be married but had lost my love. He paid better attention, seeing that I had become an adult. Perhaps he, too, had suffered the loss of a dear friend, but I would never know. Our lives had been so separate that we might as well have lived on parallel universes, and there was no crossing between them. Walter finally agreed to take me after Sunday dinner.

Walter had bought Father's little baby blue Volkwagen Beetle, which Father had driven to spite his brother and business partner who had no children at all but drove a Mercedes. I never knew what made Father decide that and when it was alright for him to match his car to his social standing in the merchant community by buying an Opel Kapitaen. Walter didn't drive fast - he flew low. At every turn in the road, and there were countless fairly sharp curves, I jammed into him or hit the flimsy door. It was a busy road, for townspeople loved heading to the hills on most any weekend. It didn't take long to find the right house in the little village of Rhoenhausen, where Frau Kramer lived. I told Walter to wait in the car and went to ring the bell. The woman who opened the door was unmistakably Leon's mother; she had the same facial features, only her hair was gray.

"Hello! I'm Stephanie," I said.

Frau Kramer's eyes opened wide, she smiled and said, "You're Leon's betrothed, aren't you." I nodded. "I hoped you would come." Then she led me to the living room and gently pushed me down on the sofa. She went to a cupboard and brought a small silver case to show me. She opened it, and in it lay our rings. "Go ahead, take it," she said with an encouraging smile. I took my ring and put it on my finger. My eyes filled with tears, and when I looked up I saw that her eyes had filled also.

"I'm so glad you saved it for me; I was just devastated when I lost him. I still have his letters, but the ring... it tells the world... you know what I mean."

"Yes, I do. Leon called me one day and told me about your engagement. But I don't know much about you and how you met. So tell me everything." We talked a long time. Suddenly, the doorbell rang; Frau Kramer opened the door and found Walter on the stoop.

"Oh dear, I forgot about you," I called out.

"How much longer, Fanny?" He sounded irritated.

"I'm ready." Then I turned to Leon's mother and asked if I might come and visit again.

"Yes, do," she said. "I'd be hurt if you didn't." Then she smiled again, kissed me on the cheek, and we said good-bye.

I had always slept so soundly that I could be carried away in my sleep and not wake up. It worried me that it might happen on my first day of work. I had a wooden chair beside my bed, a chair with a thin wooden seat. I placed our only alarm clock, which had a very loud ring, on this seat, knowing that it would make quite a racket when it went off in the morning. That, and my fear of being late, woke me up perfectly at six-thirty on Monday morning. By seven I was out of the house on my way to work. No one else was up yet. Father's office was just one floor below our apartment, so there was no need to get up before seven o'clock.

My walk to the factory took twenty-five minutes. I could have taken a bus, but I preferred walking. It was a kind of discovery journey for me, something I enjoyed very much. And it was not a superfluous activity. I wanted to see everything, every house along the way, every building and green space and unusual sight such as the ancient witches tower from the middle ages. None of it was new to me, yet children, including me, do not really see anything when they run through the streets. We never walked anywhere. But now, as I walked with purpose, everything I saw seemed to be new.

I made it right on time. After introduction to the staff of the export department, the supervisor showed me where I would do the filing. It was not new to me, and I didn't mind this menial job. It kept me out of the house and I would earn my own money. The factory had a canteen where a standard lunch, the same for all, was served. After lunch I often went walking in the neighborhood. When the weather was too cold or too wet I joined the girls from the typing pool in their large office. Then the company offered me and several other junior staff members of the export department the opportunity for French lessons, provided free of charge by the factory. So I took French lessons.

On the following Saturday Ulla and I went dancing at the German-American Club at the army base. I didn't feel much like dancing; Leon was still very much on my mind. But I had to get out of the house, and dancing was as good an activity as any, and better than some. I could at least pretend to be dancing in Leon's arms. Since I hadn't been at the club for some time, Frau Mueller, the chaperone, recited anew the rules we were obliged to obey. The purpose of the club was simply to give GIs a chance to socialize with girls, and for us girls to further our English skills. We were not allowed to leave with a GI or meet one of them outside the club. When someone asked us to dance we had to accept or sit out. We could not refuse one and then turn around and dance with another one. That was bad manners.

Ulla had done the forbidden thing once, had developed a relationship with one of them, even became engaged to be married – so she thought. But her so-called boyfriend had been a real cad. He had managed to talk her into having sex just before his tour of duty was up, and he had left the country without a word or farewell.

We promised ourselves and each other that we would obey the rules. And we did.

Four months went by during which time I walked to work every day except for a rare day when I took the bus to avoid being late. Monday nights I sang with the church choir, Tuesday nights I had French lessons, and most every Saturday I went with Ulla to the Club; if she could not go I went alone or took in a movie. Walter took me to dances and other social gathering of the Hiking Club of which he was a member. And Paula took me along on events by the Alps Club of which Werner was a member. Some evening I just went to help her with the babies, and she was glad to have me around – even as a buffer, I sometimes felt. Werner was no good with babies; he had no patience and was sometimes nearly abusive to them. With my own income I was able to buy what I needed, and it gave me great satisfaction. Leon was always on my mind, and whenever I met anyone new of the opposite sex I compared him to Leon, but the new guy never measured up. I began to fear that I would never be loved again, or that it would take years and years for me to find someone like Leon.

In late August, on a Saturday late afternoon I went swimming in the river while Hildi, who didn't like to get into the river, watched my clothes instead. The Hanfurt river is not very wide and many people liked to play there. We brought a blanket along to dress and undress underneath.

No one else was present that day. I enjoyed being the only one frolicking in the soft natural water of the river. On the upstream swim the water tugged on my swimsuit, so I pulled down the bodice altogether, allowing the sensuous flow of the waves to caress my breasts the way Leon had done. When I tired of the upstream swim I turned around and floated downstream at great ease. Being alone with nature and in nature always gave me a sense of connectedness to the All, yet I could not have named it.

Hildi was getting restless, just sitting there and watching my clothes. With a sigh I left my heavenly realm and proceeded to get dressed under the blanket, rather glad that no one else would be watching the heaving contortions of my blanket mountain. After I was dressed again we went to the Italian ice cream parlor. We ordered at the counter where four Italians, family members I thought, swooped down on us as one, eager to fill our orders. Then one of them brought it to our table, a small ice cream parlor table with a couple of chairs. On the next table sat two GIs. One could always tell Americans, even if they wore civilian clothes. For one thing, they were always young. The style and fabric of their clothes were different, certainly less conservative, and I had even seen one in a shirt that resembled a German pajama top. Many of them had crew cuts, and they chewed gum with their mouths open. And they had a way of walking that was different. They ambled along as if they had no goal in mind, their bodies seemed lose, or lax, and they often had their hands in their pant pockets. My father, a veteran of WWI, who liked a correct and smart form in everything, abhorred it.

When the two GIs had finished their ice cream they asked us if we could tell them where they might find a hotel nearby. I answered their questions as best as I could, feeling very self-conscious about my poor English. But they seemed to understand. I figured that this question was just a ruse for starting something with a German Fraeulein. Eventually, one of them, tall, dark and handsome Charley, asked me out on a date. I accepted.

Seventeen Years Later

Part II

Dagobert. There it was again. That name. Dagobert. Something in the movie we were watching on television made me think of it. The first time I had heard this name was long ago, during sixth grade needle-work class. Everyone had taken turns reading from a book about this Merowingian king who had been murdered at a young age. And something about that story had gotten under my skin and had never left me.

"Have you ever heard the name Dagobert?" I asked my husband, Charley, who stirred from his outstretched position on the sofa.

"What?"

"Dagobert. Have you ever heard that name?"

"Can't say that I have." He sat up and looked at the clock. It was half past ten.

"Let's make love tonight," he said and smiled at me.

"Okay." On our way to the bedroom I prepared myself mentally.

Afterward, Charley turned on the light on his nightstand and read in his gun magazine that he kept by the bedside. I lay quietly in the shadow of his back. That name was on my mind again. I said it silently to myself, slowly, with emphasis on each syllable, intently listening to each sound. Surely, something would reveal itself. But as always, it was in vain.

Charley's hairy arm reached over to stroke my face. "Hi, honey," he said and briefly turned his face to me. I smiled back.

Over poached eggs and sausage at breakfast the next morning, I said "I had that dream again." It was just past seven o'clock; the cannery started work early.

"What dream?" he asked.

"The one in which I'm back in school." I hadn't told him about the other recurring dream in which I'm lost inside a city, searching for a way out. Everywhere I turn I encounter blockades and war-like rubble piles that obliterate the streets. And I never find my way out.

Charley became animated. "I sometimes dream that I'm in some big public hall, and there are people all around, and I'm sitting there with nothing but a T-shirt on. I mean, it just barely covers me," and he laughed. "Then I'm supposed to get up and talk in front of everybody, and I know that when I stand up my shirt won't be long enough to do me any good," and he laughed again. "Don't let it bother you. It's just a dream."

"It's not bothering me. I like the idea of being in school again. I had always wanted to get more schooling."

"What for?"

"I don't know. Just because? But what could it mean to have the same dream over and over again?"

"Beats me," he said, wiped his mouth and went to brush his teeth. Then he put on a light jacket and picked up the brown lunch bag that I had prepared for him. I walked him to the door. He smacked the corner of my mouth with his closed lips and said with a smile, "love you."

I knew this demand and replied, "I love you too."

"Smile?"

Preoccupation with the dream had made me forget to smile. I spread my lips, and he was satisfied. I followed him with my eyes as he got into his pick-up truck and drove off to work. Charley was a tall man, and at the age of forty-one still fairly slender. He wore only sport shirts and casual slacks, and he was very proud of his thick brown hair that showed no signs of receding. A sigh escaped me. I would gladly have him bald if he would just take me out sometime, to a party, or dancing, or a play, anywhere to meet some people.

I picked up the breakfast dishes and carried them to the sink. One look at the clock, and I yelled "Sandy! Judy! Time to get going."

The girls came rushing into the kitchen just as the school bus pulled up outside. They were identical twins, very identical, and on this morning they looked exactly alike: jeans, green t-shirts, denim jackets, and reddish-blond ponytails.

"What are you up to? Trying to confuse someone?" The girls looked at each other and giggled. The school bus honked.

"Tell you later, Mom! Gotta run" and out the door they ran with their ponytails waving behind like little flags

"You haven't fed the dogs yet!" I yelled after them. Too late.

Oh well, I guess a full-time homemaker can feed the dogs occasionally, I thought. I liked being a full-time home maker. I pitied, and at the same time admired people who went to work every day, year in year out, waiting a whole year for a couple of weeks vacation which would soon be over and usher in another year of waiting. Like Charley. I was grateful that he went to work, every day, never seemed tempted not to go. He did not earn a lot of money but it was enough. I had learned to be frugal back home, and my sewing skills saved us a lot of money.

I pulled out a can of dog food and opened it. Still in my robe, I took it out to the yard where the dogs were waiting behind the cyclone fence that separated backyard from driveway. The dogs jumped and whined eagerly. They spent the days pretty much by themselves, and I felt bad for not playing more with them. Their craving for attention had become just another demand.

After I'd filled the dog dishes, I dumped the empty can in the trashcan and went back inside. I looked at the breakfast dishes, stood and stared, irresolute. Then I went to the living room, noticed my unfinished embroidery project and turned away. On a chair in the bedroom waited patterns and fabric that I had bought for new summer dresses for the girls. Above the bed was a short but wide window where a few branches from a sumac tree had grown tall enough to act as a kind of screen. The branches were open enough for me to look out, but close enough to keep prying eyes away. It gave me a feeling of seclusion, even protection. I took off my robe and went back to bed the way I did every morning.

From time to time I stirred, turned over and went back to sleep. Around eleven o'clock I began to feel the need to get up yet didn't know why. There was nothing to do. Just housework. I was tired of it. Why not just keep sleeping. I turned over again, thought about my children who went to school every day and did their duty, while I, adult Stephanie, went to bed and slept away half the day. In the recesses of my mind I could hear Mother scolding me for being lazy. With a deep sigh I got up and got dressed, and while I combed my colorless hair I studied my face in the mirror. I didn't like what I saw; there was no sparkle, not in my complexion, not in my gray eyes, not in my hair. Television ads promised that sparkle could be had if one would just buy the right product.

My neighborhood was a quiet one at the edge of a mid-size town in the Pacific Northwest. Summers were hot here, and people praised the early settlers who had planted maples, elms, locusts and sycamores, and thanks to an abundance of groundwater they had grown into majestic giants. The end of my short street made a sudden sharp turn where a clump of trees surrounded a small creek. Once past the shadow of the trees the country opened abruptly into a great expanse of tilled fields that stretched all the way to the foothills of the Blue Mountains.

I took my bicycle from the garage and rode to the end of the street and then out into the country. Winter wheat had turned the ground green. When I came to a small grassy area at the conjunction of two large fields that were planted with peas I stopped. I took off my jacket, spread it on the ground and sat down on it. The sun was already pleasantly warm though it was only April. I pulled up my knees, wrapped my arms around them and looked toward the city where I had lived since my marriage to Charley. It had been seventeen years.

Seventeen years. At the beginning, just learning the language had been a mental challenge that I enjoyed. And being in charge of my own household had given me great satisfaction and a sense of being in control. I was still in control of my household, but there was no longer any satisfaction in it, only drudgery. I needed a change. That dream about being in school again came to mind. There had to be something to a dream that kept repeating. And what about the dream in which I was trying to get out of the city. And that name, Dagobert. Why was it so much on my mind. No other name ever was, why this one. There had to be someone who could help me unravel these mysteries. Charley's parents and elderly aunt were not fit for such things. In all the years I had known them I had never heard them say a meaningful word to each other, just chit-chat.

A mental roll call of the people I knew almost made me cry. A handful of former neighbors was all I could come up with, and I knew none of them well enough or intimately enough to confide in them.

With bitterness I realized that it was the result of our many moves - on the average every two years. It had never been my idea, always Charley's. No matter where we lived, something always turned out to be a problem for him, and he insisted on selling the house. That I didn't want to move never stopped him. Once he got the idea into his head he would talk incessantly about it; he made me come along to look at houses the way he made me come along to look at cars. How I hated those trips to the car lots. And for some strange reason, the want for a different vehicle always seemed to hit him in the winter. He'd walk around a particular car, praised this or that, and expected me to agree, while I followed him around totally indifferent, shivering and shaking in the cold wind. Telling him that I didn't care about the model as long as the car would run made no impression on him.

Sooner or later I had always given in – to the sale of the house as well as the purchase of a different car. But why had I always given in, I wondered. Why had I always gone along with him, even made stupid excuses to my German family whose culture encouraged staying in one place. When we moved, I'd tell them everything about the new house was great. Two years later, I'd tell them that nothing about it was great. Why tell them anything at all, I wondered and kicked myself mentally for being so dumb. Then again, maybe it wasn't stupidity that made me tell all. Perhaps it was a kind of honesty on my part, the kind that wants to tell it exactly as it is and with enough details and background to make others understand. Yet, at the same time it was nothing but white-washing Charley's irrational behavior.

That was another matter that needed exploring. Maybe that's why I kept having the dream about being back in school. Maybe that's where I would find answers. A shimmer of hope surely lit up my face on my way back.

When the school bus returned the twins I was eager to hear of their exploits. The girls sat down at the table with their cookies and milk and I joined them.

"Now I want to hear what you two cooked up."

The girls laughed; then Sandy, the leader of the gang said, "oh Mom, you should have seen his face! See, Bobby Smith has been making eyes at me, or Judy – who knows - and yesterday he said he wanted to ask me something important. I could guess what he wanted. See, the dance is coming up, but I don't want to go with him, so I said I didn't have time now and ran for the bus. So today, we dressed alike and stayed together so he wouldn't know which one of us he wanted to ask."

And Judy added, "so he stood there, looked from me to her, and looked so helpless, and couldn't decided which one to ask, and I had the worst time keeping a straight face. I'm glad the bus pulled up then. I felt a bit sorry for him."

"Oh, the poor kid. You two have so much fun! I envy you. I envied all American teens when I first came to this country. They had so much freedom; they could chose to do and become anything they wanted."

"I'm going to be an airline hostess," Sandy said with much conviction.

"How about you, Judy?"

"I don't really know yet. But why couldn't you do what you wanted, Mom?"

"None of us could. We weren't even asked. Father owned a family business, it was all he understood, and he thought he did us a great favor by sending us to business school. Later, I managed to go to a Pedagogical Academy, but I quit after two quarters."

"Why?"

"Well, that's a long story."

Sandy finished and went to her room. Judy said, "why don't you take a class at the community college, Mom."

"A college? I can't go to a college. I only had ten years of schooling, and that was ages ago."

"But they say German education is better than ours. Why don't you try it. Just ask. And you don't have to take a full course, you can take just one class at a time. Then you'll see if you can manage it."

"But what kind of class would I take?"

"Anything you want: music, or art, or writing - anything."

"You think so?"

"Sure, Mom. Why don't you call right now – no, you should go in person. Just go to the front desk – you know where the Community College is, right?" I nodded. "Tell them you want to take some classes, and they'll help you get started. It's that simple."

"I will. You're a good kid, Judy."

A car pulled up outside and dumped packs of the evening newspaper. The girls went out and prepared them for delivery via their bikes. I sat at the kitchen table and smiled. My mind had noticed a door in the wall behind which I had lived for many years. Perhaps I could open it. Maybe there was light on the other side. A shimmer of hope made me smile.

I decided to call first, and I did so the following morning. Could I take French lessons, and what would it cost – or is it free? – to attend classes, I asked. Yes, I could take French lessons, and it would cost twenty-five dollars per credit hour, I was told. I felt a sting of disappointment. Twenty-five dollars for one lesson! That was way too much. We could not afford it. I had to be sensible about it and give it up. And I felt proud for doing it. But the brief shimmer of hope was gone, and now life seemed more dreary than before.

Charley went bowling with a league that evening and came home late. At breakfast the following morning I told him what I had learned about taking classes. "You called the Community College? Why did you do that?" He sounded alarmed, as if calling the Community College would have bad consequences.

"I wanted to know if I could take some French lessons. You know what they charge? Twenty-five dollars a lesson. If I take four lessons, that's one hundred dollars. And I would need a whole lot more than that to learn anything worthwhile. Forget it." Charley was pleased. He went to work. The twins went to school.

After they had left I stood in the middle of the kitchen in this house that had housed us only just six months and had not yet become home. It was not to be altered or updated, it would not become a nest of my own because it, too, would be sold some day. It was quiet, and empty – so empty and so silent as if it had nothing to offer me, like a stranger who didn't know what might be expected. I stood and stared, then I turned and went to the bedroom. With robe and slippers I crawled into bed, pulled up my knees and wished that I could cry. But there were no tears.

Leon! How often had his kind and gentle nature caused me to shed tears of joy and ecstasy! And for weeks after his death I had cried my eyes out because I missed him so very much. But now, I seemed to have no tears, or my tears had dried up or were frozen. Something didn't seem to work right anymore. As I was dozing off, I heard what sounded like footsteps approaching my bed. There was no one in the house and I had locked the outside doors. I turned over and dozed some more. Again, footsteps approached my bed. I opened my eyes and looked around; there was no one present. I turned over

70

again, trying not to think about it. But once again, footsteps approached my bed. I forced myself to raise my head and open my eyes and look around to prove to myself that no one was present. No one was. But it was all so eerie that I got up.

It happened again on the following two days. I never really knew if I was dreaming or waking when it happened. After the third day I couldn't bring myself to go back to bed anymore. It was just too unnerving to hear those footsteps coming toward me. I did the breakfast dishes, did laundry, straightened up the house and then drove to the city library. I wasn't sure what to look for. In the past, I had taken out biographies of prominent historical people. As I walked these familiar aisles my eyes caught sight of the name Cayce, Edgar Cayce. I had heard of it. I took it down and discovered that it was a book about the meaning of dreams. How very convenient, I thought, that I find just the thing I need. Someone is pulling strings for me, I thought and checked it out.

As soon as I got home the phone rang. A lady from a charity organization called to ask a favor.

"Do you know Renate Schulze?" the lady asked. "She's German. You are German also, isn't that right?"

"Yes, that's right. But I don't know Renate Schulze."

"Would you like to meet her?"

"Sure, why not."

"There is more to it," the lady continued. "Renate has tried to commit suicide recently. She was found in time, and she's doing well now – physically, that is. Emotionally, I think she could use a good friend. Could you see yourself nurturing a friendship with her?"

"I think so. As a matter of fact, it would do me some good, too. I don't have a lot of friends myself."

"Oh, that's wonderful – that you're willing to help, that is. I will give Renate a call and let her know about you. And you can call her, or go to her house, or however you see fit to meet with her. Is that okay with you?"

"Sure. Just give me her phone number and address." I wrote them down and said good-bye. As I sat down with the library book I wondered about the promise I had just made and hoped I wouldn't regret it.

There were chapters on all sorts of objects, or situations, or people that appear in dreams. On page eighty-eight I found a chapter on houses and buildings, including schools. I read it eagerly. And then, a shout of "aha!" escaped me. Just as I thought - dreaming of schools is a sign that further lessons are needed or wanted.

The phone rang again. Grandpa Brandon was on the line asking me to take him to town the following day. He wanted to pay his three-month health insurance premium at his former employer, the Union Pacific Railroad Company. I agreed to pick him up in front of his apartment building at eleven o'clock. I knew that Dad, as I called him, would want to have lunch, and he would invite me to eat with him. He was a rotund bald-headed man, not much taller than I, and probably seventy pounds overweight. He loved to eat out, and so did I.

I went back to reading and found that houses usually signify people, the dreamer himself. But I could not find any explanation for the meaning of a city, the city from which I'm trying to escape. If houses represent people, I thought, then the city must represent a lot of people, a whole community. Am I trying to escape from people? What people? The only ones I know are Charley, his parents, and the twins.

"Hi, Dad! How are you?" I greeted old Dad as he climbed aboard my Chevy Impala. I couldn't help giggle inwardly as I visualized him trying to squeeze into a Volkswagen Beetle.

"Oh, I'm fine," he mumbled, breathing heavily. He hauled in his second leg, then leaning heavily toward me he pulled the door shut.

"Where to?"

"First the Union Pacific office," he said, "then to lunch at the Green Apple. I'll buy you a meal." I hated this unceremonious, indifferent sounding invitation but I had learned to accept it long ago. The old man ordered the same thing he always ate – first a large bowl of clam chowder with lots of crackers broken up into it so that it was thick enough to eat with a fork. Then he had a big steak and a baked potato with lots of butter. A few green beans looked like an afterthought to the meat and potato. I ordered a salad with my steak.

"Didn't Mom want to come for lunch?"

"No," he said without taking his eyes off his food.

"Come to think of it, she never comes to eat with you. I don't remember ever picking her up with you. Oh, that's not right. Around the first of the month I take you and her downtown, but you have lunch then, and she doesn't."

"She takes a cab home."

"Why doesn't she want to eat at the restaurant? I should think she'd enjoy having someone else do the cooking for a change." I liked to deliver little mental jabs to find out what I wanted to know. But Bob Brandon was too occupied with his meal to speak. His wife, Ida, was an unusual person. She had lived in New York City but never talked about it. She had played the piano expertly without having taken more than a few lessons, but she never spoke about it. Three years before Charley she had had a baby that died at birth but she never mentioned it. She never wore bras or girdles, always slouched because it was comfortable, never exercised for her health, didn't care for fresh air, and never saw a doctor or dentist. She ate junk food and smoked, was thin as a rail and now eighty-three years old.

After I had taken the old man home I thought that since Renate Schulze lived in the same neighborhood I might try meeting with her today. I found the address easily enough. It was a big two-story house with lawns and trees and flower gardens around it. I felt a little reticent as I rang the bell. To suddenly show up at a stranger's door wasn't something I was used to doing. Perhaps Renate wasn't home. It might be better to call first. Too late. The door opened and a pretty young woman stood in the doorway and said in German with an effusive smile, "you must be Stephanie."

"That's right. How do you know?"

"Oh, I don't know," Renate chirped happily. "You look German."

"I can't argue with that because I am." We laughed. "Did I catch you at a bad time?"

"No, come on in. As a matter of fact, I was just going to make coffee. Would you like some?"

"Yes, thank you."

"Have a seat," she called back over her shoulder as she went into the kitchen.

I had expected Renate to appear, at the very least, sad or depressed looking. That was not the case. Not only did she not look sad, Renate seemed to bloom with shoulder-length curly auburn hair and a flowing floral dress. I felt dowdy in comparison in my old jeans and simple T-shirt. I wished now that I had washed my hair that morning, but as so often, I just didn't care enough to bother with it. And there was something else, something about Renate's face caught my attention, but I couldn't say what it was.

Renate came back and said, "Mrs. Reilly told me you would contact me."

"I meant to call first, but since I was in the neighborhood I thought I'd see if you were home."

"That's fine. I'm glad you came. I can use a German friend. How about you? Do you know any Germans?"

"I don't know anybody. I've lived in this town for seventeen years and have no friends. My husband doesn't take me anywhere. So, meeting you is nice for me too."

"Wonderful. I'm glad," Renate said, and she appeared quite happy. How come she's so happy, I thought. From just meeting a total stranger with whom she might not have anything at all in common except country of birth?

"If your husband doesn't take you anywhere, then you'll have to come to the country club with me some time."

"The country club! Wouldn't I have to be a member?"

"Oh no. You would come as my guest, see?"

"Oh, that would be nice. I'm so tired of fixing meals."

The coffeemaker called from the kitchen, and Renate said, "come, let's go into the kitchen. We have a cozy little breakfast nook."

During the course of our conversation I began to feel less conspicuous. I learned that Renate's husband was part owner of a family ranch, that he worked as a sales representative for an agricultural machinery company and made good money, but they were now separated. They had two sons - a freshman in college, and an eight-year old. Better yet, Renate was good friends with her mother-in-law, and the coming divorce had changed nothing in that relationship. Why would Renate want to commit suicide? Surely not because of the divorce. I wanted to know why. I always wanted to know why people acted the way they did. But this was not the time to ask. I had to wait. When I was ready to leave Renate said "Lets have lunch soon."

"Yes, let's. Any time it suits you will be fine with me. I have nothing important to do." Then, suddenly, I turned back to Renate and said, "wait a minute, I just thought of something. You said that your oldest boy goes to the community college, right?" Renate nodded. "I thought I might want to take a class or two, but it seems to be enormously expensive. What do you pay?"

"Gee, I don't really know the details. His Dad pays for it."

"They said it would be twenty-five dollars for an hour."

"You mean for a credit hour, don't you?"

"Yes, that's what they said. That's one lessons, isn't it?"

"No, Stephanie. A credit hour is one hour of instruction per week for ten weeks."

"Really? Ten lessons? I mentioned it to Charley, but he didn't tell me that." Renate kept quiet, but she had an expectant look in her eyes as though she was watching a cat that was about to pounce on the mouse. "Why wouldn't he tell me?" I wondered out loud.

"Looks to me like he wants to keep you at home," Renate said with a significant look.

"Yeah, and keep me from going anywhere," I said, and opened the door, deep in thought.

"Let me know what happens!" Renate called after me.

"I will, I will." I got into the car but didn't drive off. I sat and thought. And the longer I thought, the more upset I became. I thought about all the times that Charley had managed to deny me something without ever saying 'no.' He had done it when I wanted to join the church choir, when I wanted to see a play, take a vacation of my liking, chose the color of the paint for the next house-painting job, buy new furniture with my own money that was an inheritance from home. "Don't take any money out. Let's save it," he had always suggested, so sensible, so levelheaded. And I had always agreed. But when he wanted to buy golf clubs, or a camera, or guns, then I had been allowed to take money out of savings. But the worst of it was, I suddenly realized - and it drove the tears into my eyes - every variation of the unspoken 'no' had been accompanied with the phrase 'I love you." Even worse - if that was at all possible - it had always included an implicit demand for me to tell him that I loved him, too. He demanded that I love him all the while he suppressed and controlled and disregarded me. A cry of pain escaped me.

I had to be alone. There was no church with open doors in this town, so I drove out into the country to the spot where the two pea fields meet. I sat down there; I sat and thought, not noticing anything, just sitting while the inner storm, brought on by pain, disappointment and outrage, had transmuted into resolve to make changes. It was time that Charley learned that I was not his to do with as he saw fit; that I was a person in my own right with my own wants and wishes, likes and dislikes. And, I figured, it probably wouldn't hurt the girls to know and understand it also.

Charley was already at home from work when I returned. He sat on the sofa, watching the afternoon cartoons on television. "Where have you been?" he asked, and there was reproach in his voice.

"Out," I said flippantly, took off my coat and hung it up.

"Out where?" he asked more insistently.

"None of your business," I replied. A befuddled look spread across Charley's face, and I had trouble keeping a straight face. I reveled in the audacity to be indifferent toward his feelings and expectations.

"There's no supper," he said.

"Too bad," I replied and went to the girls' room. Clothes lay scattered across the floor, Sandy had her legs up on the wall as she lay on her bed with a book on her stomach. Judy was listening to music on a small radio while writing at her desk.

"Girls, pick up your clothes," I said sharply. "And don't just throw them in the wash. Why must you always throw your clothes on the floor! Couldn't you just as well throw them on your beds? Of course you could also hang them in the closet, but I guess that's too much to ask, huh?"

"What happened Mom. Where have you been?"

"None of your business. Answer my question: why don't you hang up your clothes instead of throwing them on the floor?"

"I don't know. Just habit I guess," Sandy mumbled.

"Well quit that habit and learn a new one: orderliness. You're fifteen years old, and I've told you not to throw your clothes on the floor for at least the last ten years. So why are you still doing it?" I was angry now. The girls were not used to seeing me in such a mood. They looked at each other, dumbfounded, then at me who was usually easygoing and non-demanding.

"Gee, Mom, if that's what you want, we'll do it," Judy said.

"Yes, this habit has got to change. I won't start sewing your dresses until I see a real change. Got it?"

"Sure, Mom," they said in unison as they began picking up their clothes.

"But where've you been Mom?" Judy asked gingerly.

"I went to meet a German woman. She's from Wiesbaden, that's not far from Hanfurt, my home town. Now hear me girls, I don't feel like cooking tonight, and I might feel that way more often from now on. So, fix your Dad something to eat. I'm not going to."

"Poor Daddy," Sandy said and hurried out the door.

"What's happening, Mom! Are you alright?" Judy asked.

"Well, as of this moment, I can say that, yes, I've never been better. And tomorrow I'm going to the community college and enroll in some classes." Judy looked puzzled and followed me to the kitchen where I fixed myself a sandwich.

"Looks like we're on our own too?" Judy asked.

"Yep." I said it with great relish, then I went to the basement to watch television on the second set. A little while later, Charley called down, "what about supper?"

"Ask the girls or do it yourself," I yelled back. Charley came downstairs, looked at me suspiciously and asked again where I had been.

"I told you, it's none of your business. But you might as well know that I went to meet a German woman today and we hit it off real good."

"So why didn't you cook supper?"

"Because I don't feel like it."

"I love you," he said gingerly, as though to calm my unusual mood.

"I'm not going to answer that any more. Now let me watch my show." Charley stood, not knowing what to do or say. After a few moments he went back upstairs.

After the girls had gone to bed that night, I was ready to confront him. "Do you know what I discovered today?"

Charley had dozed off on the couch the way he always did when watching television. At the sound of my voice he looked up, then he sat up and said, "what did you say?"

"I said, do you know what I discovered today?" Charley looked alarmed. I thought this a strange response since I hadn't even told him yet what it was.

"What did you discover?" he asked. His eyes were wide open, his posture prepared for fight or flight. I had never seen him so alert.

"I discovered that the twenty-five dollars for a lesson at the community college was meant for a credit hour, not one individual lesson. Why didn't you tell me that?"

"Oh that," he said, and his body relaxed, and he lay down again. "I didn't know that. I never went to college."

"Your father went to college, your cousin went to college, some of your classmates surely went to college, and you want me to believe that you didn't know it? You lied to me! You probably lied to me lots of times. You've been keeping me under your thumb for years. You claim to love me. Every day you tell me that you love me, yet it's all empty hogwash. Your actions tell a different story. But I tell you this: from now on, things are going to be different. I'm going to do as I please, when I please, and if I please." At the word if my eyes must have spewed utter contempt. "You have been playing games with me. That's over. I'm not your slave, I'm not your door mat, and I'm not Mrs. Charley Brandon. I am who I am: Stephanie. Tomorrow I'm going to the community college and enroll in some classes. And one more thing: stop calling me honey. I want you to call me by my name." I didn't wait for a reply, turned and went to the bedroom.

Charley came in a little later. He sounded timid when he said, "look, honey, it's ok with me if you want to take classes. I don't mind."

"What did you call me?" I said sharply.

"I mean, Steph."

"What did you call me?"

"All right, Stephanie. You can take lessons, it's alright with me."

"You should have told me that fifteen years ago. It's too late now. I no longer need your permission." With that I turned to the wall and tried to sleep. But I couldn't. That door in the wall through which I had imagined myself going was wide open and beckoned to me. Behind my back lay Charley, a silent irritant whose very presence prevented me from relaxing. My mind wandered through the last seventeen years and unearthed more and more evidence of his controlling behavior. Why hadn't I noticed it before? It was as if something had prevented me from seeing him clearly, till now. But why now? What was different now?

I was too upset to sleep. I got up and went to the basement and paced. I paced and cried, and the more I paced, the deeper my agony became. It was as if my pacing stirred up all the painful memories of my entire life. Unknowingly, I had stowed them away in my subconscious mind where they could not hurt. It had been an instinctual form of self-defense that I had never been aware of. But the time of reckoning had come, and it shook me to the core.

As I walked through the large glass doors at the community college I felt as if I had entered a different world. I read every sign that I came across but understood nothing. People were coming and going, and not all of them looked like students. Finally, I approached a woman behind a counter and told her that I wanted to take classes but didn't know how to proceed.

"What you need," the friendly middle-age woman said, "is an advisor who can explain everything to you."

"Oh, that sounds good," I replied and was quite relieved.

"Let me see who is available right now," the woman said and picked up the telephone. Meanwhile, I looked around. The building was fairly new. It was made of concrete, had fairly large open spaces that were partitioned into smaller areas by what appeared to be movable walls. Nothing, as far as I could see, had recognizable geometric shapes. It caused me, who was used to squares and rectangles, a strange sensation. But it also excited the senses.

The woman called from her desk that Dr. White was available and would come to get me momentarily. And so he did. He was a short stout man with thinning gray hair and glasses. He asked me to follow him to his office that was just around the corner from one of those moveable walls. Behind it I found not a regular office but a space, irregular like all the others. He motioned me to sit on one of the two chairs that were available beside his desk.

"I am Dr. White," he said and reached to shake hands with me. "Welcome. I'm one of the advisors. I'm told that you want to take classes here at the community college, and I'm glad to hear it. We have a fine school. So, tell me about yourself and why you want to go back to school."

"I just want to learn. There are so many things that interest me, and so many questions without answers. And I really would like to understand why people act they way they do."

"Aha," he said with a knowing smile. "Do you have a transcript from your high school?"

"No, I'm German and never went to high school. I only have ten years, and the last three of those were business education. Is that a problem?"

"As an American you have to have a high school diploma. But we know that Germany has an excellent education system. Besides, having lived out in the world for a number of years certainly counts for something, doesn't it," he said and smiled at me. "So, I see no problem. But it's too late for you to enter the Spring term and too early for Fall term. I would advise you, though, to take the College Survival course. It's a one credit course given during the summer. For someone like you who is totally new to our system it would be just the right thing."

"Whatever you say. It sounds good to me. Just wish I could start sooner."

"In the meantime, you can take our catalog home with you and look through it. Since you have many interests it would not be wise at this time to pin yourself down to a particular subject. Here is another consideration: are you hoping to earn an income with what you learn, or is it just for your own enrichment."

"You're right. It has been a rather sudden decision on my part, although my dreams have been bugging me for a long time. I need to give it more thought."

"Your dreams?" Dr. White asked.

I filled him in on the recurring dreams I had. Dr. White, a psychologist, suggested we talk about my dreams as part of my summer term. Then he handed me a copy of the fall catalog and a syllabus of the College Survival course.

"Should I enroll right now? I asked.

"It's a little early yet. Come back in early June."

I thought about it for a moment. Then I asked, "can you help me figure out my dreams? There's another one I keep having, and – oh – there's that weird thing that happened to me recently. I really, really need to talk about it."

Dr. White smiled apologetically. "I won't have time during the rest of the quarter, and then I'll be gone for the rest of the summer. I'm afraid it'll have to wait. But if you don't want to wait, I can recommend someone." He reached into his desk drawer and pulled out a business card. "Here," he said. "I know Dr. Baumgartner personally. He is an excellent psychologist and hypnotist in private practice."

"Thank you so much," I said, utterly delighted that my questions were producing such quick and easy answers, as if this community college existed for no other reason than to help me. Before I left, I asked about the fees and was told what I already knew – twenty-five dollars per credit hour.

I hurried home and couldn't wait to open the catalog to check out its contents. When I found the page with the subject listings I became quite excited. How would I ever decide among all those offered courses. I felt like a kid in the candy store.

For the next few days, the first days of May, things between me and Charley were uneasy. It seemed to me like the time when we were first married, when we had moved into our first little house together. It had been a new situation for us, and we had to sort out the chores that each one would perform, what amount of money Charley would give me for groceries and such, who would pay the bills; but most of all how to be with one another on a daily basis. I remembered that it had felt as though Charley was a guest in my home. Not only did he seem to be a guest, but he was also the sole breadwinner and, according to my upbringing, the master of the house and the head of the family. But Charley had been an only child, never had to share anything, including space. No wonder I had played right into his expectations from day one.

"We need to talk," I said to Charley one day.

"What's there to talk about?" he said brusquely. "You will do as you please from now on. You said so yourself."

"We need to talk about our marriage," I said, and before I could go on, he burst out, "you want a divorce huh?"

"Who said anything about divorce! I want to talk about the reasons why I had that outburst the other day. You need to understand what I discovered about myself and about you – and us."

"Look, you made it perfectly clear that you are going to do what you want from now on. There is nothing to talk about." He got up and headed for the bedroom.

I called after him, "for one thing, I need to know how you feel about it!" The bedroom door slammed shut behind him. I sat dumbfounded. I was willing to be open with him and try to work things out so that we could continue living together because I had promised to love him for life.

Once in bed, I said, "I promised to love you for life when I married you. You promised the same thing. Now I need you to show me that you care by opening up so we can work through this problem."

"I don't have a problem," he said. "I bring home the money and provide for you and the girls. If that doesn't tell you how I feel then nothing will. I can't do more than that. And if that isn't good enough, too bad. Good night." Charley turned out the light.

I lay quietly, thinking. Moonlight shone through the sumac tree and created a quivering light and shadow show across the opposite wall. A slight breeze brought the fragrance of lilac into the bedroom and stirred the soul with desire. It could have been a beautiful night of drawing closer to each other with love and understanding. Instead, the slight rift of a few days ago was growing into an abyss.

When Renate called one day and invited me to lunch at the country club, I was glad for a change of scenery. I washed my hair, put on make-up, and wore my best dress and jewelry, pantyhose and high heals. I met Renate in the lobby, and for once I felt like an equal to her, who always seemed at ease no matter where she was. It gave me confidence. And once again, I noticed that inexpressible something about Renate's face. We were ushered into the dining room and sat down near the window.

"I'm glad you called. I really need to talk to somebody. I hope you don't mind."

"No, not at all. I know what it's like."

"I confronted Charley about his lie. He claimed he didn't know what a credit hour is. Of course I don't believe it, and I told him so. Anyhow, that night I realized all sorts of things he had done to me over the years, controlling things. Everything had to be done his way, I couldn't even – oh God, I can't talk about it. I'm gonna cry again." I pulled out a hanky and kept it in my hand. After I had composed myself, I continued, "I sat in the basement that night and cried so hard that I got a sinus headache. I never had one, but that night I learned what they're like. It was bad. Anyhow, I told him that

84

from now on I would do whatever and however I wanted. Of course, I don't mean that I would totally ignore him now, or anything like that. So, I thought we should talk about it, but he doesn't want to. He doesn't have a problem, he says, and so he doesn't see a need to talk."

After the waitress had taken our orders, I asked, "how was it with you?"

"We were never really happy right from the start. I met Steve when he was in Germany as a GI, just like you and Charley. I got pregnant, so I married him. But I knew right away that it was a mistake. I don't know why I married him anyway. He wasn't a bad guy, and he took care of me and the boys, but we never really hit it off. We had nothing in common, I missed my Dad a lot, my Mom died when I was fourteen, and one of my brothers died from pneumonia when he was just a boy. But Steve could never understand why I missed my Dad. He thought because I had a husband I shouldn't miss my Dad. I think he resented it. Over the years, I guess, it wore him down, and me with him."

"With me it's jealousy. I'm not sure that he's actually jealous of me, but I'm pretty sure he doesn't trust me. Never, really, totally trusts me. Maybe that's why he wants to keep me at home. Or else he doesn't take me out because he thinks I'll embarrass him. I used to embarrass him, you know." And I rolled my eyes with an expression of such long-suffering forbearance that Renate laughed out loud.

"So he claims anyway. And then he looks at me ever so kindly and gently, but at the same time it feels like a million miles of empty space between us. And that look, it just gets on my nerves something awful. Like I'm some kind of dummy that he has to have patience with because I just don't know any better, you know?"

Renate nodded with a smile.

"Oh yes, it was bad. My clothes didn't fit right, my maternity outfit showed no butt, I have no poise, I always say the wrong thing, and on and on and on. And you know how hard it is, when you're new to the language, to always have the right word on hand, right?"

"Oh yes, I do remember that well," Renate sad with smile of recognition.

"I remember a couple coming for a visit, and in my mind, I was all ready with the 'nice to have met you' good-by phrase. And then they said it first, and I couldn't think fast enough for the right reply. And Charley would always ask 'why did you say this, and why did you say that,' and I'd feel so darn guilty for not living up to his expectations."

Renate took her napkin and with her eyebrows raised threateningly she wrung it as she would wring a human neck. "It made you want to do this, huh?" she said.

"Oh, you're so right."

The waitress brought our orders and we ate quietly for a while. A group of four women came into the dining room and Renate knew them. She greeted them with such an effusive "hi" that it seemed to trip over itself into a gushy gurgle.

"You seem so happy," I said. "How can you be so happy when you're about to get divorced."

"Oh, I've seen it coming for a long time. I got used to the idea. And besides, Steve earns enough so I don't have to go to work. I still have the boys, and my Dad is coming for a visit this summer. You'll have to come and meet him. He's a retired policeman. I just adore him."

"I'm glad for you. I don't know what I would do if Charley and I got divorced." I had finished my sandwich and put down the napkin. I stared at the crumbs in my dish and wondered what it would be like to be divorced. I would be free to do whatever I pleased. But what would I please to do! I could move to San Francisco; I had heard good things about that city. But how would I live; what would I do there. And I remembered what it was like before I met Charley, after Leon had died and all the years before I had known him, how utterly lonely my life had been despite my large family. No, I never wanted to feel that way again.

When I looked up Renate's face was turned to the window. In a moment, she turned it back to me, and there was that something again which I noticed but could not name. "Why did you try to commit suicide?" I asked. "Not because you're getting divorced, surely?"

"No, divorce had nothing to do with it. It happened before we knew we would separate. But I can't tell you why because I don't know it myself. They sent me to counselors and even a psychiatrist. They couldn't figure it out either. Then someone suggested a hypnotist..."

"What's his name?"

"Dr. Baumgartner."

"Oh, I heard of him. Dr. White referred me to him because I need to figure out a bunch of things. Is he good?"

"I don't know. He is nice enough, but he couldn't figure out my problem either. Even under hypnosis he could only take me back to a certain level and then no deeper. There seems to be something in my past beyond which he could not get me to go."

"How strange. I always thought that if you just ask the right questions, and if you just dig deep enough, then you'll always find the answer."

"Not in this case," Renate said and turned her face toward the window. And in that turning I saw that something for which I had had no words. Suddenly, I knew what it was.

"Now I know what struck me about your face."

"What? What about my face?"

"Well, there is something in it that caught my attention, but I could never say what it is. Until just now. Your mouth is always smiling, but your eyes are so sad."

Renate looked startled for a moment, then her eyes began to fill with tears. She wiped them away. Then she shifted in her chair and sat up straight. With a renewed smile on her face, a smile of obedience to her mind's mandate, she said, "let's talk about something more fun. Tell me about your twins. I had always wanted twins – you know: two for the price of one

– but I never got any. And to tell you the truth, every time I came home from the hospital I was glad that I had just one baby."

"Oh, let me tell you, it was hell when I brought the twins home from the hospital. Good God, I could never get any sleep. And Charley was embarrassed to shop for women's things, and his mother is so helpless she drove me crazy. And I was terribly depressed. There were a few days, when I first came home with them, when I never got any sleep. There were moments when I thought I'd die from heart failure - honestly. "

"Didn't Charley take some time off from work to help you?"

"Good heavens, no. And I never even thought to ask him, that's how stupid I was. Actually, it wasn't exactly stupidity; it's just that my father never did anything around the house and my mother never asked him to do anything. I just didn't know any better. Anyhow, once the twins got a little older, it was easier because they entertained each other. My mother always said I was lucky because of it. On the other hand, once they started walking, it was murder. They didn't want to stay in the playpen anymore, so I ended up chasing them around all day, and of course in opposite directions." It made me laugh now to think about it. "But now that they're fifteen, they're a lot of fun. Sandy is the dominant one, always quick with an answer; Judy is calmer and introspective. You'd think because they're identical that their dispositions are also identical. But then again, right from the start they were in such close proximity that only one could be the dominant one, I guess."

After they had paid the waitress Renate said, "let's go to a movie sometime."

"Oh my goodness, I haven't been to a movie theater, I mean an indoor movie theater since that one time, soon after I got here, when Charley took me. That's it."

"I can't believe it – one time in seventeen years. How did he ever get away with that?"

"Probably because I never demanded that he take me. Come to think of it, I never demand anything from him. I wasn't used to making demands. Back home, we girls had only duties, no privileges. So how do you learn to ask anything for yourself."

"And besides," Renate added with a prissy smile," its being selfish and therefore sinful." And we laughed out loud.

"You too? Did you grow up catholic, with the catechism, lots of nuns and priests, and lots of church services?"

"Oh, don't get me started on that; you'll never hear the end of it! And all the guilt trips they laid on us. Can you imagine what it was like for me to get pregnant and not being married? If it hadn't been for my Dad, I might have had to leave town. But my Dad was really nice about it. He didn't want me to marry Steve, though. He didn't think Steve was right for me. I don't know why I didn't listen to him."

"I didn't listen to my parents either. But I had a good excuse: they said no to everything." We laughed again. On our way to our cars, Renate called, "and we can go swimming here at the pool!"

"Wonderful!"

As soon as I reached home I called Dr. Baumgartner's office to make an appointment. The doctor, however, was on vacation and would not return before the end of May. I slammed down the receiver in frustration - foiled again. I paced up and down for a while, couldn't seem to concentrate on anything. I wanted answers. Wanted them now. I couldn't wait anymore. Finally, I took an old blanket and went to the backyard where the dogs greeted me with excited jumping and bouncing around. Charley and I had picked up Auggie as a weeks-old puppy. He was a medium size mixed breed dog with black shiny fur that was longer on the legs, around the face, and stood up like a little flag on his stubby tail. A year later we took in a spayed female of the same size but with much curlier black fur. We had named her Lassie.

I tried to spread the blanket on the grass, but as soon as one corner of it touched the ground the dogs were all over it. Laughing and scolding I tried time and time again to place the entire blanket flat on the ground; it was no use. Finally, I laid down on a rumpled pile, face down, and the bouncing, wiggling creatures stomped all over me, searching out patches of skin to kiss. I laughed and laughed, petted the dogs, and my troubles drifted away amid their exuberant displays of affection.

After dinner, while I did the dishes, Charley read the newspaper on the sofa and had the TV turned to the sports channel. Sandy sat down beside him. "Daddy, when are you going to teach us to drive," she asked. Charley dropped the paper on the floor and said, "soon."

"How soon, Daddy?"

"Real soon."

"You said that before. Now you have to set a date." Judy came in then, sat down on Charley's other side and began tickling him in the ribs."

"Oh, don't do that!" Charley yelled and laughed. "You know I can't handle that." Now Sandy began tickling him on his other side. He tried to escape, but the girl laughed and held him down by his arms, and Sandy said, "If you don't set a date, we will keep tickling until you cry 'uncle.'"

"I have to mow the lawn," he said and laughed and wriggled to get away from the twins. But it was no use.

"Tell us," Judy said.

"Okay, okay; I give up. How about Sunday afternoon. I'll take you to that big parking lot near the airstrip and you can practice there." The girls were satisfied, and with one more poke in the ribs they left him in peace.

Seeing Charley in such a good mood, I approached him in the hope of getting him to talk to me, or at least listen. I sat down on the edge of the coffee table in front of him and said, "Charley, can we talk now?"

"Honey, I've told you before, I have nothing to say." I resented the 'honey' but was afraid to lose his good mood if I mentioned it.

"Then at least listen to me," I replied. "When I said I'm going to do what I want I was very angry about what I had discovered. I don't mean to never cook for you again, or do your laundry and all that. I just mean that you need to consider my wishes sometimes. Remember when you wanted to paint this house, and you wanted to paint it gold because it happened to be a popular color? But I though a grayish blue would suit this type of house better. Then you painted it white. You wouldn't let me chose a color, not even just once. Why couldn't you give in to me for a change? I'm always giving in to you when you want to move again, or buy a different car or want to take money out of savings for something you want to buy."

Charley sat quietly at the edge of the sofa, his arms on his knees and his head hanging low. I couldn't tell if he was listening, and couldn't see his face. When I had finished, he stood up. His face had that irksome expression I hated so - that gentle, forgiving smile of long-suffering patience. I knew then that I hadn't reached him. On his way out of the room he said, "I have to mow the lawn."

I felt hurt. His indifference pained me right in the pit of the stomach. And, as I had always been accommodating, so now also I tried to think of what to do to make things right between us. I went to the bedroom and lay down on the bed. And I wondered why his indifference hurt me so much. Perhaps because it was the same treatment I had gotten from my parents who also had never considered my wants and wishes? But I was much older now. Why couldn't I just shrug it off? Why did I always feel the need to set things right, fix problems, make him feel good.

After a while, I took the bicycle and rode out into the country to that grassy spot between the pea fields. Under a beautifully clear blue sky and brilliant sunshine I sat and mused. No city noises reached this spot that was isolated from the city by a range of rolling hills. The only sound came from the song of a meadowlark on a fence post nearby. Why couldn't all of life be as beautiful as this graceful simplicity.

The eerie footsteps in my bedroom came to mind, and I wondered what had made them. Since there was no one there, it couldn't have been a person. A spirit would not make a noise. And if I had been dreaming, then why would I dream the same thing three days in a row. Was it the same reason, or power, or energy that caused me to have all those other repetitive dreams?

Life became ever more strained. More and more often, Charley came home late from work, or a bar, or bowling, and I spent more and more time with Renate. The girls and their after-school activities made further kinds of escapes possible. For the most part, I did my housework as usual. For the time being, I would make no major changes.

On the fifteenth of June, a Monday, summer session began at the Community College. That morning at breakfast I mentioned it to Charley.

"The class is called 'College survival,' and I guess I'll find out all those things that American high school graduates know."

"You know what they say at work?" Charley remarked. "They say that when the wife starts going to school – watch out!"

"Watch out for what?"

"You think about it." Charley said.

"When I asked you to talk, you refused. Now you talk in riddles. You don't want to be understood, do you?"

"You just think about it."

"Why should I. Why don't you just tell me. Oh, I get it! If the wife goes to college she'll end up smarter than her husband. And the husband doesn't like it because it makes him feel inferior. Is that it?" Charley gave me a peculiar look, a look I had never seen on him before. But he said nothing. He finished his coffee and went to work. Looks like I hit the nail on the head, I thought as I cleared away the dishes.

"Good Luck, Mom!" said Judy and kissed me on the cheek. Then she headed out the door.

"Yeah, behave yourself and listen to the teacher, Mom!" Sandy said laughingly, aping my frequent words of advise to her.

"Don't I get a kiss from you?"

"Oh sure, Mom. Good luck!" and Sandy kissed me on the other cheek.

Before class started, Dr. White asked me to see him after class. Fifteen young people were my classmates. Age made me feel self-conscious, but the other students paid me no more attention than they did to each other. I was really excited. I hung on every word that Dr. White spoke and wrote down the words that were new to me.

After class, Dr. White motioned me to follow him to his office. "How did you do today?" he asked. "Do you think you can handle it?"

"Oh yes, I think so. There were a few words I didn't know, but I can look them up."

"Be sure you ask question if you don't understand something."

"I will," I said. "Do you have time for me and my dreams now?"

"Yes, I do. Go ahead."

"There's the one in which I find myself back in school. But I think that it's resolved now that I'm actually taking classes. The other one goes like this: I find myself in a city, trying to find a way out. There are rubble piles and barricades everywhere, and I cannot find a way out. I got a book about dreams, and I know now that a house represents a person, the dreamer. Is that right?" Dr. White nodded. "But what does a city represent?"

"Many houses, many people. But there is more to a city than a number of houses, isn't there."

"Yes. There are streets, cars, shops, trees, underground sewer systems, water pipes, a whole world." I looked at him with mouth agape. "A whole world. My world? My life? I'm trying to get out of my life?"

"Are you?"

"Oh my God! I gotta think about that." I sat quietly for a few moments to let the words sink in. Then I picked up my notebooks, and deep in thought I left the building.

I drove to my favorite grassy spot between the fields of ripening peas that waited for the combine to come for the harvest. Oh my God, I thought again. I'm trying to get out of my life! My life with the twins? No way! But I didn't dare think any further. I pulled up my knees, wrapped my arms around them, laid my face down and wished the world would go away.

On a very hot July afternoon Charley called from a bar and explained that he had a hard day at work and would be late coming home. I didn't mind. But there was music in the background and laughter, and suddenly I felt like having fun, too.

After I had cooked dinner for the girls and done the dishes, I called Renate. Her eldest son Bobby answered. Renate was not at home, he said. I was disappointed. I really wanted to go out but needed someone to go with me. I didn't feel right about going out by myself. But I went anyway and drove off without a destination, just out, and I ended up at the bar near the airstrip. It was still very warm outside, my car had no air-conditioning, and I was thirsty. I wanted a beer, something I didn't drink very often. There was beer to be had in the bar, but I could not make myself go inside, alone, as a woman. I sat in the hot car, argued with myself back and forth until, finally, with a forceful "damn," I got out and went to the bar. I found a small table in the farthest corner of the triangular room and ordered beer. As I sat there, I thought about my life – my life that seemed to unravel before my very eyes, and I wondered how it had come to that.

I kept staring into my beer glass, not daring to lift my face for fear of giving the impression that I was on the make. I sat and thought and stared into my beer. I had never cared much for beer, but on this very hot night it seemed to be just the thing to quench a thirst. When the glass was almost empty the waitress came, and I ordered another one. At the moment when I looked up at the waitress, I saw a couple entering the bar, and to my great astonishment I saw that it was Charley with a woman. A weird sensation, like a jolt, went through me. I watched as they sat down; Charley pulled out the chair for her. She was not very tall, about the same age as I, and she had long curly brown hair, while I kept my hair short. The woman was not particularly pretty, and I wondered why Charley was with her. Perhaps she was just a fellow employee. The day was hot, the cars were hot, it was plausible that they just came inside for a cool beer.

He treated her with the same polite attentiveness and artificially friendly smile that I was used to seeing on him toward others. Then the thought occurred to me that Charley might be having an affair. I rejected it. But the thought kept entering my mind, and I had to agree that it was plausible, because Charley often came home late, or called from somewhere that he would be late. I always thought he'd be out with friends from work. That these friends could be of the female variety had never occurred to me.

Charley and the woman were totally absorbed in each other. In my dimly lit far corner, I kept staring into my beer, hoping not to be seen by them. I needed time to think about how to handle this unexpected situation. When I heard chairs moving, I looked up and saw Charley and the woman getting ready to leave. He put his arm around her waist to guide her through the door. I thought it strange that I didn't feel any jealousy.

When I got tired of sitting and staring into my beer I left. I drove to a small lake at the outskirts of town and parked the car. The stars had come out, and the moon was peeking over the black outline of the hills to the East. I got out and went to sit on a nearby bench that overlooked the lake. It was the perfect place to shut out the troubles of the world amid the fragrance of water and wilderness; the delicate light of stars and moon; the last remnants of the riotous colors of the sunset, and the caress of a gentle, cooling breeze. By the time I got home I was calm again.

I was asleep when Charley came home, but I woke up when he climbed into bed. The clock showed that it was past midnight. I turned on my bedside lamp and said, "guess who I saw today?"

"Who?"

"You."

"Me? Where did you see me?" he asked as he rose up on his elbow and faced me. His face showed the same expression of alarm that I had seen on him once before. It was on the night when I had confronted him about his lie.

"I saw you at the Arrival Bar."

"What were you doing at the bar? You were on the make, weren't you. I thought so. Ever since you started college you been telling me about your fabulous teacher and all that wonderful nonsense he fills your head with. I shouldn't have let you go. Those guys at work were right." With that, he turned over on his other side to let me know that the discussion had ended.

I turned off the lamp and lay quietly. His outburst puzzled me. There was no defense on his part; instead an accusation against me for witnessing the offense.

"Now just a darn minute," I said loudly and turned on the light again. I sat up in bed and said, "you get angry because I went to a bar, which is what you do all the time. And you don't even see a need for explaining yourself to me? For going there with another woman?" I was getting angry now, and added, "instead, you accuse me of doing what you have done: being on the make. How dare you!"

Charley turned to me then. "Look, honey," he said soothingly, "it wasn't anything at all. She's a co-worker, and I ran into her and her boyfriend at another bar. Her boyfriend was drunk and acted like a shit head to her, so I took her out of there. We went to the Arrival Bar for a beer and to calm her down. That's all it was."

"Then why did you take so long to come home? And why did you get so mad at me?"

"I went back to the Outback after Sally, that's her name, went home. And why did I get so mad at you? Well, honey, you never go to bars unless it's with me. It doesn't look good for a woman to go to a bar alone. Looks like she's on the make, you see?"

"Don't you know me better than that?"

"Sure I do, honey. I just got upset, that's all. Promise me you won't do it again, huh?"

I almost agreed, but I caught myself just in time before playing out my usual role of accommodation, obedience and submissiveness.

"If you promise not to do again what you did," I said with inward glee.

"But I didn't do anything," he said.

"Well neither did I," I replied and chuckled inwardly. We lay down again. Something unanswered seemed to linger about, though, something that required attention. But neither of us said any more.

As I dozed off I wondered if Charley had lied again. He had done it before, and probably more times than I knew. How could I ever trust him again. We hadn't had sex for quite a while. Maybe he was getting it somewhere else. But I didn't miss it. Charley knew how to have sex, but he knew nothing about making love. Leon knew how to make love, and with this yearning thought my tears began to flow.

It puzzled me that, except for the initial little sting of jealousy or rejection, it didn't bother me much to think that Charley might be involved in an affair. I remembered a time, shortly after we were married, when Charley would once in a great while take off a couple of days to visit a big city. Alone. And I had understood that need of his. After such a trip, he had talked about it for days. Except after the last trip, just the year before. He hadn't said a word about it. Had I sensed something then, deep down inside, but hadn't let it come to my conscious mind. The dream about the escape from the city came to mind again. Could it be?

"Were you having a fight last night?" Judy asked the following morning.

"I heard something," Sandy added. "But I couldn't make it out."

"No, it wasn't a fight. Just a discussion."

The girls had been picking Strawberries early in the mornings for several weeks after school let out for the summer. Now they were taking it easy; they went swimming at the public pool or at friends' homes, or hung out at the town's only Mall. Occasionally, they rode their bikes to Grandma's house. Ida Brandon, who had groceries delivered to her house, always had some goodies for them. Or they came along when I gave grandpa a ride to downtown. The old man had a way of looking with pleasure at his pretty granddaughters that warmed my heart. At other times, one or the other of the girls took the dogs for a walk, which the dogs enjoyed as much as people enjoy traveling. With their savings, the girls bought some new clothes, not all of them to my liking. And in the afternoons they still worked their paper route. For their sixteenth birthday, on the thirteenth of September, they were planning a big party.

"Who's going to pick blackberries with me?" I asked one August afternoon.

"Up on Mill creek?" Sandy asked

"As if you didn't know."

"Oh Mom, you know what that does to my hands," wailed Sandy, and Judy chimed in.

"Of course I know. I do it every summer. A few scratches, a few black fingernails, so what! It passes. See?" and I shoved my fingers under their noses. "Do you see any blackberry residue or scratches from last year?" The girls laughed. "Well, I'm going, whether you come or not. It's always so beautiful and peaceful up there. And after picking and

98

getting all hot and sweaty, jumping into the water has got to be the best thing ever. You used to like playing in the water while I picked."

"Yeah, when we were kids."

"Oh, some day when you have kids of your own, then you'll like it again, I guarantee it. Okay, okay, I'll go by myself, and I'll eat the blackberry pie by myself, too. Well, your Dad can have a piece, of course."

"Oh Mom!" the girls yelled. "You're being mean." I laughed, took the pail and bowl and went out the door.

I couldn't help thinking what a shame it was that a person could outgrow such simple pleasures. I had put on my old sneakers, which were perfect for wading through the water. That way I could reach thickets that grew along the wild creek side and half hanging over it, in areas that no one else could get to. And I wore an old leather jacket that allowed me to reach high and deep into the blackberry thickets where the sweetest berries glistened in the summer sun. And after I had picked enough and had gotten hot and sweaty, I would jump, clothes and all, into the cool, clear water that sparkled with reflected sunlight. And I would lie in the cooling water, with my face to the sun, and relish the beautiful isolation of my own little paradise.

Later that day, while I prepared the berries I had picked for the freezer, Renate called to see if I would like to go with her to a meditation class. The word meditation evoked in me the image of silent prayer in church, meditating on the sacred mysteries of the rosary. I had prayed the rosary thousands of times and did not feel like doing any more of the same. Renate assured me that it was nothing like that, or so she thought.

"Okay, I'll try it. It doesn't hurt to learn something new. What day? What time?"

"Tuesday night, seven pm, starting tomorrow. It's at the house of the man who teaches the class. You can come to my house and then we'll go together, okay?"

"Okay. It's Charley's bowling night, but he doesn't care what I do anyway."

"How are things with you and Charley?"

"Not good. But I'm okay. I'll fill you in when I have a chance." Then I picked up the college catalogue and studied the class subjects. After much deliberation, I decided on Social Work. It included English and Psychology classes, two subjects that lured me like candy lures a child. Then I went to register and paid for it with my savings.

The teacher of meditation lived in a three-story picturesque old house that was surrounded by huge trees and dense shrubbery. Three sides of the building were surrounded by a porch, and several garden chairs on it were a friendly invite. Renate pulled the bell rope. A bright tingling sound rang inside. A few moments later a man opened the door.

"Good evening," he said and bowed his head slightly. It seemed odd to me to hear a formal greeting in this town of regular people who contended themselves with 'hi,' or 'how are you.' When I was new in the country, I had thought the latter greeting to be an honest interest in me and so, lacking friends and family, I had unburdened myself as best as I was able with my poor English. And after the visit was over Charley had regularly asked, his face expressing disappointment and annoyance, the unanswerable question: why did you say that.

"I'm Dagobert Royce, your meditation teacher," the man said. I nearly jumped at the sound of that name. My mind raced with questions, but I had to wait.

Mr. Royce appeared to be in his seventies, a slender man with long gray hair that was tied in a ponytail at the nape of his neck. His face was shaven, his deep-set gray eyes shone bright. He wore loose linen pants and a loose shirt that was open at the neck.

He invited us to follow him and led us through the living room to a smaller room in the back of the house. Several comfortable chairs and a sofa stood against the walls. Beside some chairs were small tables, some of which displayed boxes of tissue.

"Make yourselves comfortable; I expect four more people," he said just as the doorbell rang, and he left the room.

"Wow! Renate! That name of his. I've been puzzling over it for years. It's from a book we read in school, and it was called 'Dagobert's Crown.' It just drives me nuts because I feel some connection to it. But for the life of me, I can't figure out why or what."

"Maybe meditation can help."

"Really? How would it do that?"

"I don't really know. But look, here they come."

Dagobert Royce came back into the room with two young couples. The young men seemed awkward and ill at ease, as if they were more at home on farms and in trucks. They wore jeans and checkered shirts, and one even wore cowboy boots. Mr. Royce asked that those who were present introduce themselves to each other. And just as I had thought, John and Ted were local wheat farmers. Selena and Blanche, their wives, were homemakers. All four were in their thirties. I wondered what it had taken for the women to talk their husbands into coming to this class. Charley could never be talked into anything to do with spiritual matters, like going to church. I had managed to get him to come once. Afterward, he had complained that I sang too loud. Since I had a good voice, even had voice lessons and had sung in my hometown parish choir, it took me a while to figure out that my unabashed singing had embarrassed him because, he feared, it would draw attention to me. Like my beautiful badger fur collar on my winter coat, or the wine red winter coat with three large black pom-poms for buttons that I later had, or the red umbrella his mother used. He never came to church again.

Mr. Royce began by speaking about the meaning of meditation, its many different forms and purposes, and its goals. Learning to control the "monkey mind," as he put it, that keeps flitting from one thing to another, like a monkey jumping from branch to branch, was the goal in reaching the "still mind." And that, in turn, would lead to real spiritual growth.

He asked everyone to sit up straight and place their feet flat on the floor. "Now, with your eyes closed, chose an object, or word, or symbol, and concentrate on it. Look at it from every angle, examine its texture, its shape, the meaning of its form, what it's made of – in short: everything about it. Push away any unrelated thought that enters, see how your mind wanders and make it come back to the object of your concentration – again and again." In this manner, Mr. Royce continued with a soft, soothing voice. His demeanor was so very gentle and warm that it seemed to fill the room with a loving peace that would fill each individual who was open and therefore able to receive it.

My subject of meditation was the name Dagobert. It was a tricky choice since I had a real live Dagobert right before me. But I steadfastly concentrated on just the name and its connection to the Dagobert of long ago. Over and over again, this mental construct wanted to flee from my concentration, and countless other thoughts wanted to creep in. It required constant and difficult efforts to keep my mind on Dagobert while pushing aside any thought that was unrelated to it.

At the end of the session, Mr. Royce gave instructions on how best to practice at home. I whispered to Renate, "I want to talk to him about his name. Wait for me outside."

After everyone else had left, I told Mr. Royce about my pre-occupation with the name Dagobert. Mr. Royce knew of the historical Dagobert, that he was a Merowingian king of the Franks during the sixth century. "The early middle age was a savage time," he said, "and not much information about the Merowingian dynasty has survived. If you want to know more, you'll have to conduct your own research. The local Public library probably doesn't have much that would be helpful, but you might check with the College library. They even have a German section. You're German, aren't you?"

"Yes, I am. Do you think that meditation could help me figure out why I'm so intrigued by that name?"

"Yes, it's possible. All knowledge can be tapped into through a still mind. It's a matter of diligent practice. Will I see you next week?"

"Yes, I'll be back."

Renate suggested that we go for a milk shake at the Ice Burg. The drive-in was busy with customers, and we sat for twenty minutes before we received service. Then we parked at the curb and talked about the meditation class while we slurped ourr shakes.

Coming home that night, I found Sandy with a badly swollen arm. The girl could not tell me how or when it happened. She thought she might have scratched herself somewhere when she had taken the dogs for a walk earlier that day. At first, it just itched, but then it began to swell and was now very painful.

"Oh Mom, it hurts so much. Am I gonna die?"

"You better not," said Judy. "We have to plan a party."

"No, sweetheart, you're not going to die," I assured her with a smile. "But we better have it looked at right away. Come on."

I took Sandy to the hospital and Judy came along. The hustle and bustle of the emergency room droned on for some time before Sandy received full attention. "It's a full moon," the nurse said. "Whenever there's a full moon, we get awfully busy."

That statement made me think of a friend who went to give birth on the night of a full moon, and so many pregnant women had come to deliver that night, that the hospital had run out of rooms to put them in. Eventually, the attending physician diagnosed Sandy's swollen arm as being infected. It could be treated with antibiotics. Once we were free to go, we drove to an all night pharmacy to get the medication.

It was past midnight when we returned home. Charley had waited up, was angry and resentful, and when he saw me coming in he yelled, "where the hell have you been?" I was so surprised, I just stood and stared at him.

"Daddy, don't yell at Mom. We had to take Sandy to the hospital. She has an infection in her arm." Judy said.

"An infection?" Charley said and turned to Sandy. "How did you get that? What happened?"

"I don't really know, Daddy. I took the dogs for a walk and scratched myself somewhere. That's all I know." The girls went off to bed.

"How come you went so late?" Charley asked.

"Because I didn't get home till about ten."

"Where were you?"

"First I went to a meditation class, and then Renate and I had a shake at the Ice Burg."

"I wonder what kind of nonsense you learn at that class," he said with disdain.

"You can come with me and find out for yourself."

"No way!"

"Then you shouldn't call it nonsense."

We went to bed, he on his side, and I on my side of our king-size bed. There was room to spare between us, where the twins had often cuddled up when they were small. Now, it was just an empty space that was infiltrated only by cold air.

I hoped that he was agitated enough to continue talking. Perhaps we would stumble inadvertently into that very discussion which I had long sought, and which Charley had steadfastly refused. But he said no more

I tried again at breakfast. "Look, Charley, why don't you come with me to the class just once. You can even walk out in the middle if you want to. Just so you can see what we talk about. It won't cost you anything, and you don't have to believe anything you hear. Just to see."

Charley shook his head. "No way," he said.

"But why not? Can't you at least tell me why you wouldn't try something new?"

"No way," he repeated.

I went to the bathroom, and when I heard the screen door slam, I knew that he had left for work. I sat down on the bed; with resignation I felt the abyss between us widening. How could I ever continue living with this man. I remembered a time, when we had been married for about five years, when I had wanted to divorce him. I no longer had any feelings for him then. A great emptiness had risen between us, and there had been no bridge that I could think of, that could have crossed that great yawning gap. But divorce meant that I would be taking the twins away from their Daddy, whom they adored. I knew I couldn't do that. So I had decided to stay with him, and I had made a real effort to recapture the nature of the feelings that I had had for him when we first met. It had worked. Life with Charley had become better then. And as long as I had a way out, I continued to do my best to make my marriage work. But now I had to face the truth that I had been the only one working on this relationship, and that I could no longer sustain it. Charley was not willing to meet me half way; there was no hope then. And for the first time I admitted to myself that my marriage was over.

I looked forward to the next meditation class. I liked the calm silence of the meditation room. Mr. Royce played a tape of a bubbling spring to help tune out the sounds of the world. I pictured myself sitting on a large log that spreads across a little stream, in the bright hot sun of a clear blue sky, my feet dangling in the cool clear water, while the brook side foliage blocks out the world, and bugs and birds, little fishes and crawdads are doing their own little things. And then Dagobert entered my mind as though he belonged to my secret little heaven, and suddenly the tears rose in my eyes. They ran down my face and made it itch, and that ended my concentration. After wiping my face I tried again. I was not to be deterred.

Sandy overcame the infection faster than anticipated, and by the time school started, late in August, she was well. Renate's father arrived on the first of September. Several days later, Renate called me and invited me to come for a real German Kaffeeklatsch.

Renate's father was a retired policeman, a tall handsome widower in his mid-sixties. He got up from his chair and greeted me with a firm handshake. During our Kaffeeklatsch, I observed him with keen interest. I had had little experience with the father species, and whenever I met one I would compare him to my own father. Renate's father seemed young; and he was lively and unabashedly outspoken. I listened with interest as he talked with authority about the changes, political and otherwise, that were taking place in Germany, and how they compared to what was happening in the U.S.A. And I was delighted to see that he was interested in what his daughter and friend had to say on those subjects.

The conversation led to the subject of travel, and that led me to reveal that I would like to visit Ireland. Why Ireland? I had no idea. Something drew me to Ireland and Scotland. I loved the rugged cliffs of the coastline and the green expanse of the countryside, which I had seen depicted on many occasions. Even knowledge of the isle's stormy weather did nothing to dispel my fondness for it. On the contrary, it only drew me there all the more.

"I would love to take a walking tour of Scotland – or better yet, a horseback tour of Scotland," I said.

"Oh no. Give me a warm, sunny place any time. Like Spain, or Greece. That's where I would like to go," said Renate.

"Do you ever wonder why you are drawn to one country, and someone else is drawn to another one?" I asked Renate one day.

"No, can't say that I do," she replied.

"I love the rugged country and cool climate of the northern countries. I never feel like going to a warm, mostly sunny country. Isn't that weird? I have an old calendar with pictures of Ireland, and I feel that I want to be there."

"Maybe its simply because you are from a northern country. I mean, your hometown is surrounded by rugged hills, isn't it? You must have picked it up from there."

"I think it's more than that. One time, Charley took us to Seattle, and we got on a ferry and cruised among the Juan de Fuca islands. It was raining that day, pouring actually, and everybody stayed under cover. But I went to the very front of the ferry – I was the only one there - in the poring rain, surrounded by gray mist and gray water and far away to either side some gray shorelines of the islands – oh, I felt wonderful. As if I belonged there. Can you imagine it?"

"No, I can't. I'll take the sun any day," Renate said and laughed.

"And think of this: I can appreciate the beauty or workmanship of Chinese art, or Asian Indian art. Or take the Indian countryside, or Chinese: yeah, they are beautiful, or impressive, or whatever, but I don't feel anything for them. I don't have an emotional connection to them like the kind I have for Ireland, for instance, or Scotland, or Celtic art."

"Hm. That's interesting." said Renate. "I'll have to think about that."

Renate did not come to the next meeting because she was taking her father and the boys on a sightseeing trip through the state. "Oh, I know," she had said. "I know there's not much to see, no castles, no great churches, no museums like there is in Germany. But this is a beautiful country, and I'd like for him to see it. He will definitely appreciate the wide open spaces that this country still has to offer." Selena and Blanche explained that their husbands refused to participate. Instead, two new women joined.

Dagobert Royce began instructions with an overview of the human condition. He said that the human being has seven bodies. "Of these bodies," he continued, "the first one is our present material body. It is the densest one. The next higher and finer one is the astral body, and again the next higher and finer one is the mental body. The higher four bodies do not concern us just now. In meditation, we shift our consciousness from one body to another. When you notice your chair to be uncomfortable, for instance, your consciousness is in the material body, the one we can see and touch and feel. When you get emotional about something, your consciousness is in the astral body. When you try to solve a mathematical problem, for instance, your consciousness has actually moved to the mental body. So, now, when you meditate, observe yourself and how you respond to the result of your concentration."

After the class, I approached the two new members of the group. "Say, Lorraine, you seem to know about the other bodies. Where did you learn that?"

"From books that I found at the Theosophical Library in Seattle."

"You took out books from a library in Seattle?"

"No no - I found what I wanted there, and then I ordered them."

"Ah so. Could I borrow them sometime?"

"Sure, any time."

"That's great. Thanks."

I meditated regularly at the same time every day. I had bought a couple of tapes for that purpose, and I always disconnected the phone so as not to be disturbed. But the problem with the tears continued, and I mentioned it to Mr. Royce at the next meeting. Mr. Royce thought it likely that my meditation had opened me to a deeper level of being; that my subconscious mind had touched on something my conscious mind had forgotten. He encouraged me to continue with my meditation practice. In time, I would come to understand what prompted my tears to flow.

From what Mr. Royce had said about the higher bodies, I deduced that my consciousness must be in the Astral body whenever I cried. So, if I turned my mind to solving a problem, then my consciousness would be in the mental body, and I would no longer feel the sadness. And I wondered: is that what I do whenever I don't cry about something hurtful? That instead of facing the hurt emotionally I rationalize it away? And what is it about these bodies, anyway. And what are they made of. And what is the meaning of 'finer.'

"Mom, you gotta buy us this stuff," Sandy interrupted my thoughts and handed me a list of items she and Judy wanted for their sixteenth birthday party. It was the tenth of September.

"I have to?" I said with raised eyebrows.

"Please, Mom? Pretty please?"

"That's better. Okay, let's see what you think you have to have." I read the list and shook my head at some of the items. Then I called Judy, and we sat down together to figure out what the girls could do without, and what was absolutely essential. And, of course, it had to be a slumber party; for sixteen guests, no less.

"No girls, that's too many. You'll have to cut it down to eight. And that includes you two. We don't have enough room for more than that."

"See? I told you so," Sandy said to Judy.

"Oh shucks. It's gonna be hard to chose. Can we invite some boys?"

"As long as the total is not more than eight, and as long as they know they're not invited to stay the night – no problem. By the way, I expect you'll want to go for your driver's license the minute you turn sixteen, huh?"

"Of course, Mom! The day after our birthday," Sandy said triumphantly. "Right after school. You can take us as soon as we get off the bus. Or better yet, why don't you pick us up at school; we could go right from there!"

"I can do that, can I?"

"Would you please?" Judy giggled.

"Yes, of course, sweetypie," I said with a grin.

The telephone rang and Ida Brandon was on the line. "Stephanie!" she said. It always sounded like a command, like an order to pay attention. "Stephanie, I've been trying to get hold of you. But your phone seems to be out of order."

"No, its not out of order, I just turn if off when I meditate," I said it and instantly regretted it. Why did I have to tell her that. Ida Brandon had no understanding for anything outside her own four walls, and they were small enough as it was.

"When you do what? Oh, never mind. Grandpa wanted you to take him downtown. But when we couldn't get hold of you he was forced to take a cab."

"Sorry about that. It might help if he called me the night before he wants to go."

"Well, we'll see."

"And I'll soon be starting classes at the Community College. They are morning classes. But the hours vary from day to day. So, if he would check with me in the evening prior to the day he needs me, we'll work something out."

"How do you expect to take care of your husband if you go running off to college?"

"Don't you worry. I take good care of Charley."

"I'm not so sure," was the reply, and then Ida hung up.

I knew she was annoyed, but I wouldn't let it bother me; being bothered by Charley's moods was enough bother. There had been times when I had wanted to say something to her, not nasty, not offensive, just to clarify a point, or let her know that such and such was not appreciated by me, her daughter-in-law. But Charley had always insisted that I do or say nothing that would rock the boat. And so the boat had never been rocked. But the smooth surface of our relationships was deceptive.

Charley called his mother from work almost every day, even if or when we would visit her that very same evening. At dinner that night, I asked him if his mother had said anything about me going to college.

"Well, yeah; she's worried that you won't have time for me."

"And did you assure her that I will?"

"How should I know that? Maybe you won't have time for much else anymore. Maybe I'll have to take my clothes to the cleaner, and that'll cost money."

"Oh! She'd like that just fine. Remember when I washed your new jacket for the first time? She said that it should have gone to the drycleaner."

"Well, she's an old woman. Don't say anything."

"By the way, does she ever ask you if you take good care of me?" I asked it jokingly. But right away, I wished I hadn't said it, because it would cause bad feelings between me and Charley. When I gave birth to the twins neither Charley nor his parents had brought me even a single flower during all the five days that I was in the hospital. At the time, I didn't think much of it. But much later I had realized how sadly Charley and his family had neglected me. From time to time, I had mentioned it. It made Charley angry. He never understood that I simply wanted to hear him say that he was sorry for his thoughtlessness, and that I wanted my feelings of pain acknowledged. But Charley always took it as a personal affront.

"Yes Daddy, does she ever say anything like that to you?" Judy wanted to know. "I don't think she likes Mom very much."

"Of course grandma likes your Mom."

"She said the other day that Mom should stay at home," Sandy added.

"You just misunderstood her, that's all. Now, who wants to go practice driving after supper?"

"That's right, ignore my question. But it won't do us any good, you know," I remarked.

"Stop it already," Charley said, trying hard to keep a pleasant expression on his face.

"What do you mean, Mom?" Judy asked.

"Oh, nothing, Judy. Don't worry about it."

"But I do worry about you and Dad. I think something is going on lately."

"Are you getting divorced?" Sandy asked straight out. It nearly knocked me off my chair.

"Oh, bite your tongue," I said and looked angry.

"What's the big deal! I know lots of kids at school whose parents are divorced."

"Well, we are not getting divorced," Charley said. "Your mother has college on her mind, and that has upset things around here."

"Don't you want Mom to go to college?"

"She is doing it whether I like it or not."

"And do you like it – or not?" Sandy persisted

Charley had finished his meal. He got up from the table and said, "I'm going to mow the lawn."

The twins were high school Juniors now. Their birthday had come and gone and with it the successful completion of their much coveted drivers licenses. College had started and I enjoyed it tremendously. I was surrounded by people who had ideas, could answer questions, or, if not, direct me to where I could find the answers. I welcomed every new thought or idea; it was as if my mind had been starved for many years and now opened itself eagerly to people and knowledge. I wanted to share with Charley the things that excited me, but he resented this intellectual influx from outside his comfort zone. Yet not talking about college life only served to widen the gap that had long existed between us. Charley became suspicious of my silence, the way I had suspected Charley's silence after his last trip to Seattle. But Charley didn't want to hear about college, what I was learning, or what the teachers had said. His parents were equally disinterested. So, I opened myself only to the twins. And the twins' interest in college life, which they intended to pursue one day themselves, helped to make up for Charley's lack of it.

Thanksgiving came, and I prepared the turkey dinner as I had done for several years in a row. Charley picked up his parents early that afternoon, and the twins entertained them while I was busy in the kitchen. Charley and his Dad liked to watch the football game on television. Even though I had not much in common with my in-laws, I nonetheless enjoyed their company on family occasions. Charley was more at ease then, and seeing a look of pleasure on grandpa's face as he observed the girls gave me pleasure as well. The talk turned to the old times then, when the town was even smaller, when the snowmelt flooded the town, when grandpa played college football and built a cabin in the mountains. The Brandons had no more family in town, and I, coming from a large family, enjoyed keeping track of Charley's dead relatives by way of reminiscences. A picture of rural life in the West emerged then through accounts of their exploits during the depression, run-ins with bears, fishing trips that yielded huge salmons, grandpa's army days in France by way of New York, where he had met Ida.

I continued to practice meditation diligently. But every time my tears flowed and a great sadness came over me. Trying to identify this sadness became an obsession like the name Dagobert. And then came the day when my concentration became so deep that I thought I felt a presence, the presence of some one being. A longing arose in me to become one with this presence, and suddenly, the words, "come to me," escaped me. And then, as if my sadness was becoming too heavy to bear, something broke my concentration.

I scoured the nearby College library and found bits and pieces of information on the Merowingians. I learned that the Dagobert of my fascination was Dagobert II, the grandson of Dagobert I, an esteemed ruler of the early Franks. Dagobert's father had died young, and evil people had coveted the child's crown. The Bishop of Poitiers had taken the boy for his safety to Northumbria where he was raised as a son of king Alkfrid. Later on, for greater safety, he had been sent to St. Erk near Slane, a small community of monks near the river Boyne in Ireland.

Now that I had gained that knowledge, I wondered what it was good for. It still didn't tell me anything about his end, the murder that had caused me to fixate on the story and on Dagobert in the first place. I had to find the book again, the book of which I only knew the title, but not the author. I had tried it a couple of times when I was visiting back home in Germany. I had checked at the school where I first learned about it, and at the State library that happened to be located just three blocks from my family's home. I had even checked the local College Library's German section, just in case. And I had requested by mail that family members and friends search for it. But all had been in vain.

But in my searches, I came across a local bookstore that I had always wanted to investigate but never did. It offered many spiritual books and other paraphernalia, some of which seemed to me the gushy output of melodramatic personalities. But the book 'Man Visible and Invisible,' authored by a man named Leadbeater, was a title that aroused my interest. It promised to supplement what Dagobert Royce had taught in meditation class, and I bought it.

I took my college assignments very seriously and studied conscientiously. I spent much of my study time at the college library, where I didn't feel as isolated as at home because hours could go by without any human interaction. And if I didn't understand something, there was always some teacher or other who could help me. Finals week came and went, and I had earned an A in every course. I grinned from ear to ear when I told the girls about it.

"Oh Mom, we're so proud of you," said Judy and hugged me.

"Did you pick a program yet?" Sandy asked.

"Not yet. I'm just taking some basics, like English and Math, and Composition. Oh, and computer! I want to learn to use a computer. Writing essays and compositions will be easier than using this old typewriter. I make a lot of typos, and erasing them is a real headache."

"When are we going to get one?" Judy asked. "You know, we're about the only kids in high school who don't have one?"

"Oh, I doubt that very much. There are plenty of people who are too poor to buy one."

"What does it cost?"

"I have no idea. Why don't you find out."

Later that evening, Sandy asked, "Daddy, did you know that Mom got all As?"

"No, I didn't know. She didn't tell me," Charley answered indifferently.

"Well she did. What do you think about that?"

"It's great honey, just great," Charley said without looking up from the newspaper.

"And she's going to take more classes, aren't you, Mom?"

"Definitely."

The girls went to their room, and Charley said to me, "instead of spending money on yourself, I think you should save the money for the girls' education."

"You're saying I shouldn't go to college?"

"Yes, that's what I'm saying. What for, anyway? You're not going to start a career at your age. You're a housewife, that's your career."

I felt as if a bucket of ice water had been poured out over me. All the joy and enthusiasm of going to school, of learning, had suddenly soured. I wanted to say something, lots of things, objections and accusations and explanations, but I was too stunned. And what was the use anyway. I knew I would not be able to sway Charley, because hc felt that changing one's mind is a sign of being weak. So, I remained silent. I did my chores. Then I dressed warmly and drove out to the lake where I could be alone. Charley had taken me fishing there during the first year of our marriage. Very early in the morning on opening day, when it was still dark, he had taken me. Since it had been a new experience for me, I had enjoyed it. But once the girls had arrived, these fishing trips had ended for me.

There were no fishermen now, whose voices drifted across the water like a gentle wave; no meadowlark sang now to embellish the silence; no horseback rider came by to remind me of my own yearning for horseback riding. Why had I given up that dream, here in the US where many people keep horses, I wondered. I had wanted to visit a dude ranch, where I thought to experience the ways of the old West, but Charley had said no. Why had I never fought for anything I wanted to do.

All I had ever dreamed of had been squashed, first by my parents and then by Charley. And to my astonishment, no, to my horror, I realized that Charley had done it with no more effort than simply saying "no." And I had submitted without the slightest effort to get what I wanted, had never put up a fight. Why?

I sat, and sat, and watched the ducks performing their antics on the lake. Black cloud rags hurtled along the mountain tops and colored the bare trees black. Their branches reached high into the sky, and they were as black as the crows that quarreled among them. A cold breeze forced my blood to the surface of my face, but my body remained cozily warm. I closed my eyes to better feel the caress of air across my face. Leon had caressed me with that same gentleness. I thought that this must be what's meant by 'being present in the moment.'

Suddenly, the answer came to me; the answer to why I had never fought for what I wanted. But then I realized that I had, indeed, fought for what I wanted during the time when I knew Leon. First, it had been a running away from Mother who said 'no' to everything. But eventually, I had begun to say what I wanted and acted on it. But once I was a married woman, being obedient to my husband was necessary in order to validate my role of being a good wife. Being a good wife – and by extension a good mother - was the only value I possessed. Oh God! For the first time in a long time I cried for myself.

Charley's words, that being a housewife was my career, rang in my mind. It made me want to scream with rage. I had always been glad that I didn't have to go to work every morning, but had I simply been hiding at home? If I had something exciting to do, something to do with languages, or being an airline hostess, or if I owned horses and could go riding, oh, how I would love to do those things … the tears came again. And some day the girls would be in college, and surely be married later on. Most likely, they would move away from this small town. What then? Charley's words that being a housewife was my career, sounded in my mind like a prison sentence. If he had his way, for the rest of my life I would be a housewife. Oh God! The wife of a house! -

A sudden gust of wind carried off my cry of agony. I pulled out my handkerchief to drown out my sobbing. Suddenly, I noticed someone standing beside the bench I was sitting on. I looked up and saw a man who looked down at me with much compassion. He was dressed like a fisherman, but had no fishing gear.

"Did I startle you?" he asked gently. I shook my head. " I'm sorry to intrude, but I hate to see anyone so unhappy. May I sit down?"

I wasn't sure what to make of this situation. Should I be wary of this stranger and leave? Then again, he seemed to enjoy this place as I did, or he wouldn't be here.

"Sure," I answered and moved over a little.

"My name is Dagobert," he said and reached out to shake hands.

I couldn't help laughing as I shook his hand and said, "My name is Stephanie. Forgive me for laughing, but this is just too weird. I have an obsession with the name Dagobert, and even though it's an old and rare name, you are now the second Dagobert that I have met in this out-of-the-way town."

"I'm glad you're laughing now. Wouldn't it be nice if all of life's troubles could be made to vanish with laughter."

"True."

"Do you come here often?' he asked.

"Whenever I need to be alone. But it's getting colder, and darker. I think I better go home. You've been very kind, thank you." While I reached for his hand my eyes searched his face. It was a rugged yet handsome face with deep-set eyes that shimmered with serenity. For an instant, I felt drawn to those eyes. It confused me. I shook his hand quickly and hurried to the car. Once inside, I sat for a few moments to collect my thoughts. As I was leaving, I could see that the man remained sitting on the bench.

I will have a career, I thought all the way home. Then I said it out loud so that I might get used to the word 'career.' During my youth, that word had a slightly shady meaning. Since good women stayed at home, took care of husband, house and children, it was implied that women who had a career were selfish. It made me feel sad to think of all the thousands, even millions of women for whom a career would have been a needed form of self-expression. Yet they were not allowed to pursue a career. God only knew how many millions of children bore the brunt of their mothers' frustrations.

I understood now that my marriage had ended, if not legally then certainly emotionally, even if Charley did not know it. It relieved me of the burden of feeling responsible for Charley's happiness. I felt much freer, lighter, and therefore happier. Gone was the anxiety of how to reject his advances without feeling guilty. The fact that Sandy had said, "what's the big deal; lots of people are divorced," freed me from the anxiety about what I perceived to be a threat to the girls' happiness. Besides, there was no hurry. I would do my thing and let Charley do his. Meanwhile, I would study and learn, so that I could stand on my own two feet when the time was right for the split.

I requested a consultation with a career adviser, and we discussed my options. The field of languages drew me, and being an interpreter seemed to promise an excursion into international fields. Would I be able to find work in this agricultural town, the counselor mentioned. Probably not. But I might not always live here. And with a computer, much could be done via the Internet. And with the knowledge of foreign languages, diverse fields would have opportunity for employment. For now, I would take the basics. Later, I would switch to a four-year college – and that prospect excited me tremendously – where I would select a major. So, nothing to worry about for now. And time would provide answers.

I made a lunch date with Renate to fill her in on the changes that were taking place in my life. We met at a little coffee shop on Main Street. Renate was waiting in a booth.

"I used to be the first one to arrive because I never had anything important to do to make me late. You know, for the first time, I feel like I have arrived in the world of adults. People my age have experienced so many different things that I hadn't, and I always felt left out, or behind the times, and it made me feel insecure and ignorant. Even Sandy's infection of her arm was a new experience for me, and that's why I liked it. Can you believe that? You know what I mean, don't you?" Renate nodded with a smile. "Things are different now."

"You even look different," Renate said.

"How?"

"Well – happier."

"I am. I have discovered that my marriage is dead. Oh, I have discovered a lot of things. About myself, too. By the way: I think I understand how meditation works. I mean, I think I can put it into words. One can tap into knowledge when the mind is still, Mr. Royce has said. And when I go to the lake, actually, it doesn't have to be the lake, just anywhere I can be alone, where it's quiet and private, yeah, then the mind becomes still. All I do is observe what there is to see, not thinking, just observing, and then, quite suddenly, an answer to a question that might have been on my mind for a long time suddenly pops into my head. It's really uncanny, the way that works. And looking back, I can see now that I've always done that, even when I was just a little kid. But nobody taught me that."

"It's as if you always knew it."

"That's right. And how would I know that?"

"I have no idea."

"I think it's something I always knew, subconsciously. I think it's knowledge from a previous life time."

"Aha! You believe in reincarnation."

"I'm not sure. I've never thought about it very much. But you know how it says in the Bible that we should become perfect 'as my heavenly Father is perfect?' Well, how could we possibly do that in one life time? Maybe that's why we are reborn many more times, so that we can learn all that we need to learn."

"It would make sense, I guess," replied Renate. "But why would you remember this part and no others?"

"I don't know. But maybe I do remember many other things and just haven't noticed it yet. Besides, there is so much to learn about that stuff. But hey, tell me about yourself. Your divorce must have been finalized by now."

"Yes, I'm glad it's over. I get alimony and child support, and if I'm not extravagant I should be able to live okay. Steve can see the kids any time, so we have no problem with that. But now I have a different problem. Robby, my eight year old, wants to spend Christmas with his Dad. He adores his Dad. I don't mind, basically; on the other hand, I want him at home with me for Christmas, too. We could, of course, split it up: Christmas Eve with me, Christmas Day with his Dad. But cooking a big dinner for just Randy and me is no fun. And Steve's Mother will be with Steve, of course. On the other hand, I could invite my friend," and now, Renate smiled gleefully," to dinner. Randy wouldn't mind, I'm sure."

"Your friend?" I asked. "A boyfriend." Renate nodded.

"I've known him from the country club. He's a few years older than me, but he's really nice. And he owns his own business, so he can be very generous." And while she continued to talk about the man in her life, Renate smiled effusively, but I noticed that her eyes were still sad.

"Why are you looking like that?" Renate suddenly asked.

"Like what?"

"Like – oh never mind." She seemed glad to be interrupted by the waitress who took our orders. Then we compared notes on husbands and children, on life in Germany and life in the US, on Christmas here and there, and all the little Christmas things of our youth that had given that holiday its individual and very special character.

"I remember my first Christmas with Charley really well because it was so different from what I had expected. He went to his company's Christmas party and came back half drunk. And he brought home a gag gift. I was really steamed to see him half drunk. You know what a Christmas party in Germany is like: Advent songs, coffee and Christmas cookies, poetry, totally pious. And Charley brings home a gag gift, a dirty one at that."

"Oh wow! How come you didn't go with him?"

"It was just for employees."

"Spouses are always invited to those events," Renate said.

"Not at the cannery."

"Oh sure they are. Always. But I'll check with somebody I know, to make sure. I bet you anything that wives are invited, but your Charley didn't want you there."

"Because he thought I would embarrass him," I finished. "Or maybe he's afraid I'll find out something about him that he doesn't want me to know. He forgot his lunch once, and he wouldn't let me bring it to him. And they didn't have a cafeteria then. But you know what? I don't care anymore."

"Good for you," Renate said.

As we were leaving, I asked Renate if she would be coming to meditation class again. "I don't know," said Renate. "I'm not really getting much out of it."

"Oh, I think you should, specially since you never understood what drove you to do – you know what."

"But even the hypnotist couldn't find out."

"You might have a chance with meditation. And I found a great book: 'Man Visible and Invisible.' Would you like to read it?"

"Yeah, I could. I'll come by some time and pick it up, okay?"

"Any time between now and January. I should be home most of the time. Merry Christmas, Renate!"

"Merry Christmas!"

I had a dream that night about the house in the country that we had once lived in about ten years earlier. I had loved it there, but, as always, Charley had found reason to leave. It wasn't the first time I had dreamed about it, but this time, I saw a pile of firewood by the fence, but on the neighbor's side of it. There had never been a firewood pile there, only a sheep pasture. I couldn't let go of that discrepancy.

I had learned from one of my books that while the material human body sleeps, the spirit body pursues its own interests. On a sudden impulse, I left the cookie dough I was working with and headed out of town to that house and acreage I had come to love. To my great astonishment, there was indeed a pile of firewood right where I had seen it in the dream. A newly built house on what used to be sheep pasture explained the existence of the firewood.

I sat in the car and stared at the firewood pile. I reasoned that this couldn't be a premonition of a future event because the event had already occurred. And if my spirit body indeed pursued its own interest, then it must have gone to see what was happening at the place that I loved. What was most amazing about it, though was the fact that my waking mind had retained the dream. Oh, my goodness, I thought, if the waking mind can retain knowledge from the spirit body's nightly activities once, then it must be able to do it again.

And it had, I suddenly realized, and it send shivers down my spine. Several times over the years I had dreamed about the convent boarding school in Venusbrunn, the place I loved more than any other place, even my hometown. In several dreams I had seen little changes taking place, such as the appearance of lay personnel that had never existed before. And in the last dream I had seen a deep trench being dug in the torn-up park. Sometime later I had found out from an old school friend back in Germany that the school had been sold to the city who had torn it down to build a new school.

The girls came home from school and found Christmas cookies cut out on a cookie sheet, and more dough in the bowl, and the oven preheated, but no mother. They were worried, but since there was nothing else to do, they finished the baking chore. When I got home all the dough had been made into cookies, and the girls sat with them at the table and ate as though there was no tomorrow.

"Oh no! they're for Christmas, not now!" I yelled when I came into the kitchen and saw what the girls were devouring." I snatched the cookies and put them into the cookie jar.

"Mom! Where were you?" They literally yelled at me.

"I had to check something out," I answered, sat down at the table. "Thanks for finishing the cookies. I had to leave in a hurry."

"Why?"

I filled them in on what I had discovered.

"Oh, I love it," Judy said when she had finished. "Do you think that could happen to me, too?"

"I really think that anybody can experience things like that. Just depends on your openness to matters that are beyond what we classify as normal, things that are not easily understood. One thing I'm absolutely sure of is this: there's more to being human than meets the eye." Then I sent the girls to the basement so that I could hide the cookies till Christmas.

One of the few things that Charley was willing to discuss was Christmas gifts for the girls. He loved his daughters; he was proud of their academic achievements even though his own had been pretty poor. And he appreciated their good looks and very feminine proportions. He broached the subject of Christmas gifts after the girls had gone to bed. I suggested that we buy a computer.

"That's much too expensive," Charley said and suggested something sensible, like clothes.

"I really do want one, though," I said when Charley gave me a funny look, "I admit that I want one for myself, yes. Writing papers is so much easier that way. And then, once we're on the Internet, you can find all sorts of information about all sorts of things. Remember when you wanted to know where you could find a certain gun to buy? You can find that out on the Internet. We could make it a sort of family gift."

"If I say 'no,' I suppose you're going to buy it anyway, huh?" I thought for a moment. My first impulse was still to please Charley. It was a long-standing habit and would take time to break completely.

"Yes, I would. But it would be so much nicer if you would agree. And maybe you could find out from some of your co-workers where one could buy a computer without shelling out too much money."

"Hmm," Charley said, and it was not clear to me what it implied. I considered asking him about his company's invitation to the annual Christmas party but decided to forget it. I didn't care any more. Instead, I told him about the dream about the wood pile, just in case it could create a common interest for us. Just coincidence, he said and turned his attention elsewhere.

One week later, on the day before Christmas Eve, Charley came home from work with a big smile on his face. He came in through the side door, and laying his finger on his mouth he motioned me to be quiet and follow him to his pick-up truck. He opened the passenger door and pointed inside. I looked and discovered a large box that contained a computer. I was thrilled and kissed him on the cheek.

"Where can we hide it?" Charley asked.

"Take it to the laundry room while I occupy the girls in the living room."

Once I heard him going downstairs, I followed him. I opened the box and took out all the paperwork to study it later. Then I piled some dirty laundry and bed sheets on top and around the box until it was fully concealed.

"That was the best surprise ever, honey. What made you decide to buy it?"

"I thought it would be good for the girls to learn how to use one of those. They will probably need it some day. And you can use it too, of course."

"You're so right," I said and turned to go upstairs. Charley followed me; he put his hands on my hips and moved them slowly to my front, and by the time we reached the top of the stairs, he said, "let's make love tonight."

"Okay," I replied. But I didn't mean it. I wanted to say that I had a backache, or a headache, or any kind of ache. But how could I reject him just now when he showed himself willing to do what I had asked for. I went to the bathroom and shut the door. I pulled down the toilet cover, sat down, and closed my eyes. In my mind, I brought up the face of the man from the lake, Dagobert, who had eyes that shimmered with serenity. And I wished that I could drown in those eyes. They seemed to promise the fulfillment of what I had been yearning for all my life. Yet I could not name the object of this life-long yearning.

Six months later I hat completed my first year at the community college. Three days later, the twins completed their junior year in high school with a three-point-nine and three-point-seven grade point average. Pride and joy reigned in the Brandon household. Even Charley grudgingly admitted that I had done well, and he proposed to celebrate with a dinner at the Mission Tower, a prestigious and expensive local restaurant. I looked at him with wonder; he had never taken me out for more than hamburgers or Chinese food. Charley saw my reaction, and he smiled.

"How come?" I asked.

Charley put his arms around my waist and looked at me with an expression I hadn't seen on him since the early years of our marriage. It was an expression of total attention, with eyes meeting and not in a hurry to go somewhere. "Well, honey – Stephanie," he said. "I've been listening to the guys from work, talking about their wives and the troubles they have. I mean, I've heard it all before, but it began to dawn on me that I might have the same trouble some day if I didn't pay a little more attention to you, huh?" With that, he kissed me gently on the cheek."

I was utterly bewildered, but put on a smile, a dutiful spread of my lips. Charley, an only child who was used to thinking of himself first, and often only, did not notice the insincerity of it. Instead, he drew me even closer and said, "I hope it isn't too late."

Panic rose in me. Now he cares, I thought. After he ruined our marriage! I don't want to anymore! Tears of anger and disappointment welled up in my eyes. Charley was dumbfounded. "What's the matter, honey?" he asked.

"Nothing. I don't even know why I'm crying. It's so stupid. Just don't worry; I'll be alright," I said and hurried off to the bathroom. I wiped my face, wiped my nose, wiped my eyes, but the tears kept coming.

"Come on honey! It's time to get going," called Charley through the door.

"Okay, I'll be right there." I forced myself to be calm and quiet, and told myself to appreciate the nice thing my husband was doing for me.

"Are the girls ready?" I called down the hall to where the twins' room was located.

"They are ready," they called with one voice and stepped out into the hallway.

"Oh, I know what you're up to," I said with a big chuckle, seeing the girls in identical outfits and hairstyles. "Trying to confuse Grandpa again, huh?"

"He's so cute when he looks at us so utterly befuddled," Judy said, and the girls laughed at each other. Then they went out to the car and I followed slowly. I was trying to give myself time to undo what crying had done to my face. When we arrived at the Mission Tower, the girls took the car and went to pick up their grandparents who were to join us.

While we waited, Charley and I had a cocktail in the lounge. Charley even asked me to dance with him, something he hadn't done in years. "I'm glad now that you are learning things," he said. "Someday, you might even get a job and earn money. We could use that for the girls' education, or save it for our retirement." I felt a sting at the mention of 'our retirement.'

"Or we could travel," I replied. The music stopped, and we sat down. "Wouldn't you like to see other parts of the country? Or Germany. You liked it there. Don't you ever want to go back and see it again? You would enjoy the sights so much more as a civilian. You never talk about traveling."

"Probably because I never think about it. But I've always wanted to have a hock shop." He said it with a look of delight, as though he had just tasted a delectable morsel. Seeing a puzzled look on my face, he added, "oh, I know, it's nothing spectacular, but I just like it."

"A hock shop? How come you never mentioned it?"

"Because I couldn't give up a steady salary for something as uncertain as a hock shop." He had always been a good provider, I thought, had always brought home the money. I was astonished to hear that he had put off his own dream for the sake of his family. Yet, I was also annoyed at the revelation because I was now dreaming about a future that did not include him. But as his wife who promised to love and support him, I felt that I owed him something. What lousy timing!

"What do you like about it?"

"I'm not sure. Maybe it's the antiques that I would come across, or the kind of people that I would meet. Or maybe it's just the dealing and wheeling."

"Well, when I complete my education and start working, you can do it."

"You wouldn't mind then?"

"No, of course not."

Someone entered the restaurant. I looked up and saw, beyond Charley's shoulder, a man. He was alone. The waitress seated him nearby, and when he turned around, I saw that it was Dagobert, the stranger from the lake.

"What's the matter?" Charley asked. "You look like you've seen a ghost."

"Really? Hm. I don't know." Then I focused hard on Charley who was talking about something or other; but I heard nothing. I yearned to be with the man who was sitting just two tables away. But he might as well be sitting on the moon. I was glad for the distraction the girls caused when they came in with Ida and Bob.

Judy was upset with Sandy for not giving her a turn to drive. The day before, Sandy had gotten equally angry with Judy for the same thing. I shook my head and said, "I'll be glad when driving becomes a chore instead of fun for you two. Then maybe we'll have peace." And turning to my in-laws, I said, "Hi Mom, hi Dad. How are you?"

"Confused," mumbled Bob Brandon with a chuckle.

"I don't understand why you can't tell them apart," said Ida with a shake of her head. Then looking to the girls, she pointed at one of them and said, "You're Sandy." Then, pointing at the other one, she said "and you're Judy." It sounded more like a question than a statement. "Am I right?" The girls laughed, Charley and I laughed. Pretty soon Ida laughed too, a short, almost silent laugh while she looked around and enjoyed being laughed about.

"Right," said the girls in unison.

Suddenly I remembered that Ida never ate at restaurants. Now, perhaps, I would find out why she didn't, and I watched her carefully. Ida wore that same non-descript smile that I knew from Charley. It was not aimed at anyone or anything in particular, but seemed to float about benignly, indifferently, and quite impersonally. Ida's salt-and-pepper gray hair had grown nearly down to her shoulders. She had a sallow complexion on her delicate, narrow face. I knew from photos that Ida had been very pretty in her youth, with a slender body and reddish blond hair. But Ida's slightly bulging watery gray eyes had always repulsed me. Bob, on the other hand, broad and stout in body, and fairly bald, always seemed content. I wondered what it had taken for the old man to convince Ida to come along

"Well, tell me Mom, did Charley complain to you that I neglected him because I go to school?"

"Of course I didn't," Charley fell in.

"But I'm asking your Mom. Did he, Mom?"

"Charley doesn't complain; he's a good son," she answered.

"Maybe he didn't complain because he had nothing to complain about," I suggested.

"Well, in my time, women stayed home and took care of their husbands."

"It's alright Mom. I don't mind that she goes to college."

"Grandma, you gotta go with the times," Sandy said. "Do you have any idea what it costs to go to college nowadays? Mom could get a job and help pay for it."

"Well in my time, if you didn't have the money you didn't go to college," Ida said.

"But dear, sweet grandma," Judy chimed in. "You have to have a college education nowadays or you can't get a decent job."

"All right, you guys, lets not get all worked up about this," said Charley. "Let's just figure out what we want to eat."

All this time, I had tried hard to keep calm. But just knowing of Dagobert's presence and keeping my eyes from wandering was very stressful for me. While everyone was immersed in making a selection from the menus, I looked over toward him. He was just then looking toward me, and our eyes met, and I felt a shiver going down my spine.

I can't do this, I thought. How stupid can I get – I don't even know the guy. For all I know, he could be a miserable wretch that I wouldn't want to know. But those eyes! Forget it. I'm going to concentrate on this dinner and my family.

I said I would like a glass of wine, and Charley ordered it, even for the girls who were only seventeen. Ida thought it inappropriate, Bob said nothing and just smiled, but Charley said, " you know, it doesn't make sense that teenagers can go to war but can't even have a beer."

"You should have seen Charley, when he discovered wine in Germany," I said. "He thought it tasted like water, so he drank too much and too fast and ended up under the park bench. But that's before we knew each other."

"Don't talk about that," half-whispered Charley to me. "I don't want the girls to know about it." Ida's smile shifted a little at the thought that I knew something about her son that she had never known herself. But she kept on smiling.

"What's the big deal," Sandy said. "Lots of kids drink beer and smoke. If they're too young, they'll find someone who's old enough and will get it for them."

"Yeah, and they offer it to us, so we could drink or smoke if we wanted to."

"Well I hope and trust that you don't," said Ida who did both.

"Grandma, you don't have to worry about us. We'll wait till we are twenty-one, okay?"

Ida looked puzzled for a moment, as though she couldn't decide if she was being made fun of or not. When no giggles followed the remark, she was satisfied.

The waitress came then and everyone ordered steak, except Ida who said she wasn't very hungry and would just have some dessert later on. Aha, I thought, just as I suspected. Her teeth are bad.

Despite myself, and when I thought to be unwatched, I stole an occasional glance toward Dagobert. He ate his meal in silence and alone. When he left, I was disappointed for having lost the chance to find out something more about him. But I was also glad to be rid of his distracting presence.

The summer months dragged on with extreme heat. I had never gotten used to it. The house had no air-conditioner.

By evening the heat that had accumulated in the attic seeped down into the living space and prevented the house from cooling. Drained of energy, I dragged myself around, many chores went undone, then I felt guilty for being lazy. The only relief was in the water. I liked to swim, but the public swimming pool with its chlorinated water that burned my eyes, with nothing to do but swimming back and forth, did not lure me. Mill creek on the other hand, was much more fun. I would climb down to it by the end of the bridge and then wade some short distance away from it to a bend in the creek. There, all sights and sounds of human activity were obliterated. The water that came down from the mountains was cold and clear. Little fishes nibbled on my toes and tickled them, and all sorts of other little creatures swam and crawled by, and the flow of the water caressed my body, and the deeper pools allowed for continual swimming against the current. By August, blackberries glistened in the sun most invitingly; but those berries which had lost their sheen were the ripest and sweetest, and I ate all I could reach. Then I would lie in the flowing water, enwrapped by the silence of the heat that caused all life outside the water to take a siesta. In those hours, I felt as if I were the only human being anywhere. Instead of feeling alone I felt at one with All.

Classes started for Sandy and Judy in late August. I had the house to myself again and resumed my regular meditation practice. Knowing of the higher bodies and their function, I practiced shifting my consciousness from the astral to the mental plane and was thereby able to avoid the tears.

Then I noticed a change in my dreams. The dream about being in school no longer happened, and I was proud to have discovered its meaning. But now, my dreams were stories; entire stories with minutest details that took place anywhere in the world, with all sorts of people, under any circumstances. Not only that, but the dreams about people came in sequels, like the continuing saga of some prominent family. Suddenly, I remembered Dr. Baumgartner, the hypnotist. I had forgotten about him. I called his office, and as luck would have it, he had a cancellation that very afternoon. I went to see him.

The doctor's office was located in a modern one-story brick building. The receptionist had me fill out some forms. I asked the price of a session, when it was quoted to me a gasp escaped me but I agreed. I didn't have to wait long; the doctor, a tall slender man with graying temples, ushered me into his office and invited me to sit in one of three comfortable looking chairs. The famous couch stood further back.

"How do you do, Ms. Brandon," he said with a pleasant smile. He was dressed in normal street clothes, and he looked at me carefully from behind steel-rimmed eyeglasses.

"I'm fine, thank you."

"First, tell me a little bit about yourself," he said. I had noticed in the past, with dismay, that I could talk endlessly when I felt the other party to be truly interested. I was careful not to get carried away with my life's story.

"And what brings you here today?"

I told him about my dreams, about my obsession with the name Dagobert. "Your name isn't Dagobert, by any chance?" I asked and couldn't help laughing. No, it was not. Then I explained to him the dreams that baffled me, how very involved they were and unbelievably vivid and detailed, and I mentioned my very own soap operas of continuing sagas. Then I asked him to hypnotize me if he thought it would help.

"It is certainly possible to find answers that way," the doctor replied. "But there seem to be two things going on here: on the one hand, it's your obsession with the name Dagobert, the king. And you want to know why that book made such a lasting impression on you. And then, there are your dreams which are trying to tell you something; messages from the subconscious mind about your waking life." I nodded, almost jubilant because I would find some answers. But it would not be so easy.

Dr. Baumgartner suggested the self-guided form of hypnosis that might bring to light some answers. I would be

132

awake at all times, but still able to tap into deeper levels. For that purpose, he offered me the couch where I made myself comfortable. He sat down on a chair nearby. With a calm and soothing voice he led me to visualize a broad stairway leading down into a beautiful garden with many flowers and a path leading through the flowers. He waited and asked what I saw, and I described a wall to the left, a wall that looked like a castle wall I knew from home. Then I wanted to follow the path that led around a large evergreen shrub, and after I had turned the corner I saw a meadow against a background of woods that were part of the castle grounds. And suddenly, I heard myself calling out, "I could have been an artist."

I rose abruptly. Tears were in my eyes and running down my face. After I had calmed down a little, I related to the Doctor how I had taken a drawing course in the sixth grade, how my class had gotten permission from the castle authority to enter its woods to observe real live deer for the sake of drawing them. And I had done a very good job of it. But my parents had never taken notice of anything I had accomplished or had been good at.

I left confused and disappointed. Instead of finding answers, I had discovered the memory of just another painful incident that needed to be healed. Now what. I went to the lake and returned to the same bench where I had gone many times in hopes of finding those wonderfully serene eyes again. But the peace I was used to gaining there did not materialize. I could not still my mind because the stranger, Dagobert, continually trespassed on it. With a deep sigh, I got up and went home.

The first day of fall quarter came, and I was relieved to know that my classes would provide direction and structure for my overly agitated mind. By mid-morning, between two classes, I went to the cafeteria for a cup of coffee. I sat down at a small table and began reading the first chapter of the sociology textbook. Suddenly, I noticed someone standing opposite and looking at me. It was Dagobert. He smiled as he looked down on me, with a coffee cup in his hand. "May I sit down?" he asked, just as he had done the night on the lake. I was shaking inwardly, but nodded. He pulled out a chair and sat down.

"Stephanie, isn't it? How are you?" he asked, still smiling.

"Fine."

"Are you surprised to see me?"

"Yes."

"May I ask what you are studying?"

"Sociology."

"You look at me as if you were seeing a ghost," he said. "I'm not a ghost. Touch my hand, see?" he pushed his right hand across the table toward me. It was a slender hand with long slender fingers and clean fingernails. I stared at it, numb with bewildering emotions. I did not touch his hand.

"Perhaps I should let you study," he said, and the smile vanished from his face. He got up from his chair.

"No, no - stay," I finally managed to say. "I don't mean to be unfriendly. It's just that...well - do stay. It's alright."

Dagobert sat down again. I had shaken off the startling affects of his sudden appearance. He was a man of medium height and build, and his short-cropped wavy hair was the color and sheen of polished pewter. In his clean-shaven face were engraved deep furrows, and a deep tan betrayed much outdoor living or working. He might be in his early sixties, but could be younger, I thought. He was dressed in jeans and a sport shirt, wore leather shoes, and he carried a backpack over his shoulder. His deep-set gray eyes looked at me steadily; it sent shivers through me.

"Are you taking classes, too?"

"Yes, I'm taking a math class. How about you?"

"I'm just taking basics."

"You were very unhappy when I first met you. Are you happier now?"

My eyes wandered past him and through the great window to the large patio and sitting area outside the building.

A little stream, surrounded by lawns and low shrubbery, meandered through the grounds, and tall cottonwoods trees and short vine maples surrounded the site like a protective enclosure. My mind tried to decide on an answer. Why don't I just say 'yes,' I wondered. Why am I trying to come up with the absolute truth? Is he entitled to the absolute truth? Then again, I don't even know the truth myself.

"Forgive me," he said. "I shouldn't have pried. It's none of my business."

"No, it's alright. I don't mind being asked. I figure that if someone wants to know something he should ask. And if I don't want to answer, then I won't, right?" I felt more relaxed now and smiled.

"You're absolutely right."

"So, therefore, I'm not going to answer your question," I said, feeling rather playful.

Dagobert laughed. "I guess I had that coming."

I looked at my watch. "I gotta go." After a moment's hesitation, and realizing that I might be playing with fire, I added, "I'd like to see you again."

"I'll be here three days a week, Monday, Wednesday and Friday. Shall we meet here, same time as today?"

"Yes, I'd like that," I replied. With a wondrous mix of satisfaction and delight and promise of a coming adventure, I walked off, feeling light as a feather.

I had trouble concentrating on the subject of English composition. I probably had the biggest smile on my face as I sat in the last row of my class and thought about what had just transpired. I felt that this man, Dagobert, possessed the wisdom and knowledge that had always attracted me to older men. Such a person was calm and certain, did not need to prove himself, and could quietly listen to a contradictory opinions, even nonsense, yet feel no need to correct or change such a mind. And I had to end up with Charley! But it was my own fault for wanting to get away from home and missing love and affection so much that I couldn't be happy anywhere. And with a mental jolt I realized that Leon had spoiled me. He had given me a taste of love that I feared never to find again. So, I had settled for Charley who had been more affectionate than my parents had ever been to me.

The moment I came home, the telephone rang. It was Ida. Bob had fallen to the floor in the kitchen and Ida was helpless to get him up. Could I come and help her, she asked.

"I'll be there just as quick as I can," I replied. On my way, I wondered what to do; I wouldn't be able to lift him either. Charley could not be called unless it was an emergency.

Bob was still lying on the floor in his pajamas and his own excrement when I arrived. "Hey, Dad," I said, joking, "wouldn't the sofa be more comfortable?" Then I directed Ida to bring the little footstool from the living room, and while I, with my arms under Bob's arms, lifted him as much as I could, Ida pushed the little footstool under his butt. Once seated on the stool, and with me pulling his arms up and forward, he was able to get on his feet. Then I walked him to the bathroom and helped him into the bathtub. I removed his soiled clothes and cleaned him up, dressed him in clean pajamas and put him to bed. Bob, as usual, was very quiet. Once in bed, he smiled and appeared to be as content as always.

Charley went to visit his Dad that evening. "He had the flue, nothing to worry about, he reported. "That was a good thing you did, honey," he said to me.

"What amazed me most is that I wasn't at all embarrassed to see him naked and even wash and dry him in that state. I guess you do what you have to."

"I'll call Mom tomorrow and check on him."

"What if he needs a doctor. Who is his doctor anyway?"

"I have no idea. I don't think he has one."

"What's the matter with grandpa?" Judy asked.

"He just got the flue and it made him weak," said Charley. "He fell on the floor and your Mom got him into bed. He'll be fine in a few days."

136

Later on, after the twins had gone to bed, Charley said, "lets make love tonight."

"I'm going to take a bath," I said.

"What, now?"

"Yes, I'm tired. I had a big day." With that I disappeared into the bathroom. Charley could hear the water running and he went to bed to wait for me. But I did a nice, long soak with lots of pine extract. Meanwhile, Charley fell asleep.

Two days later, sitting in the cafeteria with my books, I didn't have to wait long. Dagobert approached me quietly, pulled out a chair and sat down across from me. He said nothing, just smiled and looked into my eyes, and I thought I'd faint dead away.

"You have to stop looking at me like that," I said.

"Why – what do you mean?"

"Your eyes are so...so... I don't know what to say." And I picked up my book and hid my face behind it. Then I thought it was rather childish, so I put it down with a bashful grin. Dagobert watched my antics and just smiled, as though there was nothing I could do that was not perfectly alright. "Okay, now I know what I wanted to say: you seem to know all about me by just looking at me or right through me. It's a bit unnerving."

Dagobert's eyes drifted off into the distance. After a little while, he turned back to me and said, "you're right, to an extend. Because I know human nature, I know you. But I don't know the person Stephanie. See what I mean?"

"Yes, I do," I answered and smiled because I liked the way he answered, so short and yet so to the point. It made me feel more at ease.

He took a sip of his coffee and pushed the cup aside. Then he placed his crossed arms before him on the table and looked at me expectantly, saying, "so, who is Stephanie – other than the mother of beautiful twins?"

This unexpected and very personal question made me feel uneasy. For one thing, I wasn't used to anybody showing so much interest in me. And furthermore – I didn't even know the guy. "You first," I said. "Who is Dagobert – other than the man who saw my beautiful twins?"

He laughed and said, "let's make a deal: I won't ask you who Stephanie is, and you don't ask me who Dagobert is. Agreed?"

"Fair enough," I said and we shook hands on it. Then we talked a little more about nothing much, this and that, until it was time for me to get to my next class.

On my way home, I went to see grandpa. He was sleeping when I arrived, and Ida was concerned about him. He had no appetite, something that Ida could not view as anything but bad. She gave him plenty to drink, but he refused to eat.

"Well, look Mom, it can't hurt him to lose a few pounds. Don't worry about it. I'm sure it's just the flue. Do you need anything for him, or for yourself?"

"My grocer brings me everything I need."

"Good. Just call me if you need me, okay?"

When I reached home, I found a message from Renate on the recorder. I called her back and she told me that she was getting married. An invitation was in the mail. How could this be, I wondered. I remembered distinctly how Renate had told me once, that the more time she spends with her boy friend, the more boring he became. And what about that statement made by Renate, that she always seems to do what is not good for her, as though she were programmed for self-destruction?

That evening, I mentioned to Charley that I thought I should talk to her about it.

"What's there to talk about?" Charley replied. "She's got to be happy or she wouldn't marry him, now would she."

"But she said herself once, that she always seems to do what's not good for her. And I fear this is another one of those times."

"Oh, you're working yourself up about nothing. Leave her be. She must know better than you what's good for her. You

138

are making too much of this."

"I don't think so. I know her, you don't."

"Well, has she asked you for your opinion?"

"No, of course not. When she told me about him being boring, that was the last time she talked intimately. I didn't see much of her afterward. It's like she didn't want to talk anymore. I thought about it for a while, then I asked, "how could someone be programmed for self-destruction?"

"I have no idea. Did you see Dad today?"

"Yes. Other than not eating, he's okay, I guess. He was asleep."

"Let's make love tonight," Charley said and smiled at me. Instantly, the long-standing habit of compliance surfaced, but I caught myself just in time. "I'm too tired," I said, got up and went to the bathroom. Charley said nothing, but I had a feeling his eyes were following me.

A couple of days later, he called for me while I was studying, to watch something on television.

"Look! Look!" he called, all excited, the way he often did. I was torn between pleasing him and pleasing myself.

When the calls didn't stop, I yelled back, "I'm studying!"

Charley stopped calling then. Later, when I put away the books and joined him in the living room, he said gravely, "you claim not to neglect me."

"That's right."

"But you do."

"Just because I don't come running when you want me to see something on TV? I was studying. I do need to do that, you know."

"I'm not talking about that."

"Then what?"

"You don't want to make love anymore. What's going on?" Well, well, I thought. All of a sudden, he wants to talk.

"I was tired."

"How could you be tired when you're sitting around with your books all day?"

"It's mental work. Take my word for it, it's tiring."

"Alright. Then you admit that going to college makes you neglect me."

"I don't want to talk about it." Seeing a look of consternation on his face, I added, "remember when you didn't want to talk? Now, I don't want to. I have the same right, don't I?"

"So, you don't care about our marriage."

"You're the one who didn't care when I needed to talk!" My voice began to rise; I felt uneasy about this confrontation because my obedient self was not used to dealing with a husband that way. I worried about the consequences. What if he just walked out?

Renate's wedding took place at three o'clock on a Saturday afternoon in mid-October. Charley was also invited but preferred not to go. He would not feel comfortable among the country club crowd, he said. I didn't mind. Charley had no suitable clothes for a wedding anyway because he didn't like wearing anything fancy. Besides, it would have embarrassed me to be seen at the wedding with a husband who didn't know how to dress properly. Worse yet, he would probably roll up his short sleeves to show off his muscles, would feel awkward for not knowing what to do with his hands, thereby making everyone around him uncomfortable. But the weirdest thing he did, and I had noticed it on other men also, he would suddenly draw himself up to his full height while at the same time pulling up his pants at the waist and tucking in his shirt. The shirt usually didn't need tucking in, and the pants always ended up where they had been before being pulled up. It seemed to me a rather offensive, albeit unconscious, act, as if the man had just finished using the toilet.

The Bride looked radiant in a light green dress of organza and lace. Little bits of baby's breath adorned her curly brown hair, and she carried a small bouquet of tiny white roses.

Her new husband, Andy the businessman, a little on the chubby side, looked grand in his black tuxedo with satin lapels. He was a nice looking man in his late fifties, with smooth everything – face, hands, hair. On this occasion I met Renate's boys, and her former mother-in-law whose friendship and support for Renate had not diminished. According to Renate, this lady was everybody's dream of a mother-in-law, as loving and caring to her and her children as she was to her own son. I wished that I could have such a mother. And Ida? A long time ago, when I was new and naive, I had thoughts of Ida being a substitute mother to me. But Ida turned out to be as self-centered and self-absorbed as her son. She never showed any interest in me or my life outside my role as wife to her son.

When I said good-bye to the newlyweds, Renate beamed with pride and joy. But her eyes were still sad. I left the wedding party with a sigh, hoping that time would still my doubts.

Old man Brandon recovered, but ever so slowly. He lost some weight during his illness, but once he was up and about he looked well enough. Ida was happy that she could feed him again. After visiting his Dad one evening, Charley told me that his Dad might have had a slight stroke. Bob had always been a man of few words, so it had taken a while for Charley to notice a little slur in his speech. Ida didn't seem to be aware.

My studies took up all my attention as the quarter progressed toward mid term. I still managed my daily meditation, though; it surprised me just how much I could get done with the help of a good time plan. I continued to meet with Dagobert between classes and always looked forward to our conversations because he could feed my mind with ideas that tantalized my sense of adventure. Throughout the years I had been married to Charley, I had learned very little because Charley knew very little. Countless times I had asked him to explain this or that, only to discover that Charley had no idea, and, what was worse, didn't care to find out. Even a movie we might be watching together, usually brought up some term or word or idea that was new to me, but Charley couldn't help because he had fallen asleep.

"Do you know what the purpose of life is?" I asked Dagobert one day.

"Yes. Do you?" he asked playfully.

"No, that's why I'm asking."

"I cannot tell you," he said with a mischievous grin.

"How come?"

"Because you have to discover it for yourself."

"Oh you!" I slapped his hand playfully, pretending impatience." That might take too much time. Why not tell me right now?"

"Because you wouldn't believe me."

"Why not?"

"Because people only believe what they already know."

"That doesn't make sense."

"Think about it: do you believe everything that people tell you? Of course not. You only believe that which makes good sense to you, what you have discovered for yourself to be true. If I tell you that five times four is twenty you believe it because it's a fact that you can check out for yourself. But if I told you that life and consciousness are two sides of the same coin you'll not accept it unless it makes good sense to you. And the reason it makes good sense is because you know it to be true even if only subconsciously."

"Oh, I see! That must be why it's sometimes impossible to convince other people of something."

Dagobert nodded. "If you want to know the purpose of life, meditate on it. It'll come to you, and then the truth of it will never leave you. Try to meditate on the two words: I am."

"I am - what?"

"Just 'I am.' Concentrate on those two words. Don't try to answer the what."

"Alright, I'll try," I said, thinking that it will be a queer thing to do.

Thanksgiving came and went with the usual family dinner that I always enjoyed because everyone was at ease. Bob joked with the twins, the twins made fun of Ida which made her laugh, Charley teased his Dad, and I was glad that everyone enjoyed the turkey, the jellied cranberry sauce, the mashed potatoes and even the red cabbage, a German tradition. There was even stuffing and gravy, something that went missing at my first Thanksgiving dinner. I had been used to roast goose on high holidays, and a goose provided plenty of drippings. My very first turkey, however, had almost none, and I hadn't known how to make gravy without it. Neither did I make any stuffing because there were no giblets and no inner organs. I had only found them wrapped in paper and stuffed into the bird after I had sliced into it. And when I had asked Ida's advise, she had said something about stove-top stuffing which had thoroughly confused me. So, on that, my first Thanksgiving, we had a turkey without stuffing and gravy. But everyone was kind and did not complain, and I had been very grateful.

Once the quarter had ended, I meditated every day. It was difficult to just focus on those two words, 'I am'. They seemed to demand an answer. But I steadfastly persisted. When I needed an answer, or find a missing connection or explanation, I browsed the book store. And as if by magic, I always came across just the right book to help me along. I gave up meditating on Dagobert for the time being; I sensed that the answer to that riddle would come to me in good time. What was it that Dagobert Royce, the meditation teacher had said? When the student is ready, the teacher will appear. It was true, I had experienced it myself.

"Can we make love tonight?" asked Charley one evening as we got ready for bed. I winced. What to do? How long could I hold him off with excuses, I wondered. I decided to simply tell the truth.

"I don't feel like it, Charley," I said and looked him square in the face.

"Too tired?" he asked gently. I wished he had gotten angry. It would be so much easier to just walk away from him.

"No Charley, I just don't feel like having sex anymore."

"Are you going through menopause?"

"That might be it," I replied, grateful that he had proposed a way out.

"But aren't you too young for that?"

"It can happen to young women."

"Maybe you should ask the doctor about it."

"I will, I will."

Once in bed, lying side by side on our backs, Charley said, "you have changed."

"Yes, I have," I answered. "I'm learning and growing as a person, and I like it. I wish you would take classes with me, or read some of the books on spirituality so that we could talk about the things I'm learning. They're so interesting. And there is so much to know and understand! But you don't care for that sort of thing, do you?"

"You're right. But I don't mind if you learn whatever it is you want to learn. I just hope it doesn't pull us apart in the end."

"People have been known to grow apart."

"I will wait," he said and kissed me. Then he turned over and left me to my thoughts. And I thought about sex. Did I really not want to have sex anymore? For the rest of my life? What about making love? Leon knew how to make love, but maybe he was exceptional. If all men knew how to make love like Leon did there might never be any divorce. Perhaps it wasn't fair to compare Charley to him.

I was annoyed with him for being kind and patient one time, and so utterly dense and stubborn at other times. I wished he would make up his mind about which way to be. Suddenly I realized that the changes in myself must have an affect on him as well. He was used to me being and acting a certain way. But now, just as he had said, I was changing. But I was not changing into a different person, just a more complete person, the person I was meant to be. I was learning and growing, but Charley didn't.

For now, it thrilled me to know that I was, finally, coming into my own. Regret over lost time could overshadow my joy if I allowed it; but I would not. Better late than never, I told myself. And certainly, my experiences of these last seventeen years were worth something. Indeed, it was no wonder that Charley would feel confused and unsure toward me. I planned to be more patient with him.

I was baking Christmas cookies again. It seemed to me that I enjoyed housework more now since I was going to college. The chores had become a welcome change from a lot of sitting and studying. I put some Advent music on the record player and hummed along as I cut out the cookies from the gingerbread dough. Then I decorated them with half a maraschino cherry in the middle and almond halves in a star pattern around the cherry.

The girls were still in school when the phone rang and Ida reported that something was wrong with Bob. "I can't get any reaction out of him," she said.

"Well Mom, call an ambulance!"

"You really think I should?"

"Is he conscious?"

"I don't know. He's acting so strange."

"Then call the ambulance. No, never mind, I'll call it myself. Hang in there. I'll be over as soon as I can." I called for an ambulance, then wrote a quick note for the twins and went to rescue Bob. The ambulance had arrived, and the medics were working with him. He had been sitting in his chair, watching television, quiet as always. It had taken Ida a while before she realized that something was wrong with him. He was conscious, but just barley, and after the medics had taken his vital signs they put him on a stretcher and took him out to the waiting ambulance. Ida was crying.

"I'm going to follow them to the hospital," I said. "Do you want to come along?"

"I'm not dressed or anything. Could you come for me later?"

"OK. I'll call you from the hospital and let you know how he's doing."

On my way to the hospital I realized just how lucky we were to have one. A neighboring town had lost its hospital due to a lack of adequate funding. But what a bummer to have this happen so close to Christmas. It could put a real damper on things. I figured that Bob had suffered another stroke, a more severe one this time. What if he suffered some kind of permanent disability? Or, worse, what if he didn't make it? Then, there'd be a funeral. Ida would not want to live alone. Christmas would be sad and somber.

I had never been around elderly people, never had to nurse grandparents because they were either dead at the time of my birth or had died soon afterward. When I arrived in the emergency room, a nurse was taking vital signs again. Bob acknowledged my presence with a faint smile. I was asked to fill out forms, and when I was done with that I waited by Bob's bedside. Asking him how or what had happened didn't get much of a reply. Bob mumbled something; I didn't understand. He repeated his mumble, but I gave up asking and just sat quietly, thinking about this man, the grandfather of my girls, who cherished the extra large dimension in everything he did and was, starting with his own girth. He had smoked huge Havana cigars before the embargo on Cuba. His last car was a 1954 Lincoln Continental; it had to be the longest one ever made. Then he discovered that it didn't fit in his garage. His binoculars were so powerful that they were useless for bird watching. He had a flashlight that was too big and heavy to be handy. When vandals disturbed the family cabin in the hills he took lumber to repair the damage and used nails that were so big they split the wood. I sat there and chuckled.

After a while, a nurse came and wheeled Bob out of the room to do some tests, brought him back, and then took him out for another test. Finally, I was able to get a little information from a doctor – it looked like Bob had suffered a stroke. For the time being, they would keep him for observation overnight. I called Ida and filled her in.

She was upset to hear that Bob would be spending the night in the hospital. She had never liked being alone, and she asked if one of the twins could stay with her. I suggested that she call the girls at home and ask them herself.

It was past dinner time when I got home. Charley had learned from his mother what had happened. Judy volunteered to spend the night with grandma. After Charley ate a bowl of cereal, he dropped Judy off at his mother's and then went to see his Dad in the hospital.

Two days later, the telephone rang, and when I heard a man's voice I fancied it to be Dagobert. By the time I had cleared this fantasy from my mind, the man stopped talking but I hadn't heard what he said.

"Excuse me, would you please run that by me again."

"This is Dr. Houser," the man said. "Are you Mrs. Brandon?"

"Yes, I am." I was getting worried.

"I'm sorry to tell you, Mrs. Brandon, but your husband passed away this morning."

"My husband passed away this morning?"

"I'm so sorry, but there was nothing we could do for him. He suffered a massive heart attack."

"Wait a minute. What are you talking about?" I finally came to my senses. "How did my husband end up in the hospital?"

"You brought him in with the ambulance, didn't you?"

"Oh good grief. You're talking about my father-in-law. Gee, what a fright you gave me."

"Oh, I'm terribly sorry. You are not Mrs. Bob Brandon, then. Oh, I do apologize." There was silence for a moment as I tried to take in what had happened. Then Dr. Houser asked for Ida's phone number to let her know that her husband had passed away.

"No, you better let my husband tell her the bad news in person. I'll call him at work and let him know."

"Again, I'm sorry for the mix-up."

"Good-bye," I said and hung up the phone. I sat down, still slightly numb from the shock of hearing my husband had died. Someday he would; men most often die first. A jumble of feelings had momentarily overtaken me at the doctor's announcement. I had to admit that among those feelings was also one of relief at being free from the problem of how to separate myself from Charley. But relief had been followed by an intense feeling of loneliness and isolation. And all of it had occurred in a flash.

I dialed Charley's work number.

"Stephanie? What's up?"

"Charley, Dr. Houser from the hospital called."

"How is Dad?"

"He died this morning, Charley. He had a massive heart attack, the doctor said." There was silence on the other end. "Charley?"

"Yeah, I heard."

"I thought it best if you tell your Mom in person."

"You're right," he said vaguely, then hung up.

I sat down and tried to absorb what had happened. Never having been overly sentimental, I figured that Bob, grandpa, was an old man, his body had given out, and dying was the natural consequence of living to a ripe old age. Nonetheless, it was a rather sad event, and telling the girls about the loss of their grandpa proved to be more difficult.

"How could this happen, in the hospital that's full of nurses and doctors, right under their noses?" Judy fretted.

"You're right, how indeed. The doctor said that grandpa had a massive heart attack and that nothing could be done for him."

"They revive people all the time," Sandy said. "People that drowned, and people that died on the operating table. Why not grandpa?" And sitting down heavily on a chair, she added, "Christmas is going to be awful."

"Poor grandma. What's she going to do all alone in that apartment," said Judy.

"There are plenty of other people in that huge building."

"Yeah, but you know grandma. She never socialized with anybody."

"So, now she'll learn why she should have," Sandy said flippantly.

"I hope Daddy doesn't take it too hard."

When Charley came home, I greeted him at the door, searching his face for signs of how he was taking the death of his father. He looked somber, gave me a hug and held on for a while, something he hadn't done in a long time. His hair, I noticed, had begun to turn gray, not at the temples, which only contributes to a man's good looks, but throughout. I wondered if the attraction of the gray temples was a sign that women liked maturity in a man. I knew that I did, and always had. When Charley sat down on the sofa, the girls sat down beside him to hear every word. He told them that his mother had cried a lot, had complained about being alone, that she could not live by herself, that she needed someone to be with her, that she was asking to move in with us or have one of the girls move in with her.

We, the women of Charly's life, let out a unanimous "no way!"

"We'll have plenty of time to think about that. Right now, I have to make funeral arrangements. I'm glad now that Dad bought the cemetery plots for himself and Mom. It'll make things easier."

On the day before the funeral, Charley called me and the girls together into the living room. "We need to talk about Mom," he said. "She already told me plenty of times that she can not live alone. She'll either have to have someone stay with her at night, or else she'll have to move in with somebody. I think she wants to move in with us."

"You have got to be kidding!" I said and couldn't help laughing out loud. "We have exactly two bedrooms. Besides, I distinctly remember, at the time when we lived in that big house on Garda street, when I said that I would gladly have them live with us if the need arose – remember what she said? She said, she would never ruin her son's life by moving in with him."

"I don't remember hearing that."

"Well, she said it to me. And I guess she never realized what that statement said about her." Charley grinned.

"We just might have to move to a bigger house."

"Oh no! Not again!" yelled the twins and I like a well-rehearsed chorus.

"I see no alternative," Charley said. "Grandma doesn't want to live alone. Would either one of you want to stay with her?"

"No. One night now and then is okay but not every day," Judy said.

"Yeah, and without grandpa, grandma just isn't any fun. All she ever talks about is food," Sandy said. " I'm not going to move," she added and crossed her arms over her chest in an attitude of defiance.

"Neither will I," said Judy and did likewise.

"I don't want to move either. I've had my fill of that," I said. "Your mother can live alone; she's not sick or feeble, and we're only minutes away."

"I know. Maybe she can get used to being alone," said Charley.

"Oh, I'm gonna miss Grandpa," Judy wailed. "He's so cute when he sits there and chuckles to himself. Grandma bought a Christmas present for him. I can just see her holding the present in her hand and no grandpa to give it to. She's gonna cry, I know she will. On Christmas!"

"Let's not cry over something that hasn't happened," I said. "For now, girls, bake some banana bread; there's a couple of overly ripe ones in the fruit basket."

The girls went to the kitchen. One pulled out the cook book, the other got hold of the bananas. While they worked, they argued about how to prevent another move; a move that would cut them off from barely established friendship circles. Their town was small but spread out far and wide because of its agricultural character. There was no public transportation, and neither stores nor shops or even hamburger joints existed within walking distance. It was wise to hang on to friends who owned cars.

Charley had become quiet behind the newspaper he was reading. When the silence lasted longer than usual, I asked, "are you okay?"

Charley nodded. Then he put down the paper, stared out the window and said, "I don't think he liked me."

"Who? Your Dad? What makes you say that?"

"Well, a number of things that I had never paid much attention to before now. Like all the times he went to the cabin or fishing but never took me. He always had an excuse."

It occurred to me that Charley might be right. I recalled Bob telling me about his first child with Ida, a beautiful boy that had died at birth because the umbilical cord was wrapped around its neck. I had had the feeling then that Bob still mourned that child. Human nature what it is, Bob probably built in his mind a larger than life image of this beautiful child's future. Charley never had a chance to live up to those expectations.

Oh my God, I thought. I had done the same thing. I had built in my mind an image of the life Leon and I would have had together. And, of course, it was a wonderful life full of joy and happiness. Charley never had a chance to live up to those expectations. Poor Charley.

"Did he ever tell you that he loves you?"

He though for a moment. "No, he never did"

"But that doesn't mean that he didn't, right? My parents never said that either."

"Yeah, I know it's not necessary to hear it said. Still…"

"It would have been nice to hear it, huh?"

"I sat by his bed side and we talked chit-chat as though we had all the time in the world. Nothing but chit-chat! Not a single meaningful thing did we say to each other. And now he's gone." Charley wiped his eyes and left the room.

How I wished he'd have shared himself more often with me. We could have grown closer instead of apart. I was grateful for the Christmas tree that spread some badly needed cheer. It was a six-foot noble fir that Charley had bought from a friend's tree farm. The girls had decorated it. I had put on the final touch, tinsel. I always took great care with it, placing one strand at a time, so that the up-and-down space between the branches was filled with it. After dark, I'd sit without benefit of eyeglasses to blur my vision. Then I'd watch as the airflow from the furnace stirred the tinsel and reflected thousand fold the tiny white lights. It made the tree look like a sky full of twinkling stars. Sheer magic. I could never get enough of that glorious sight.

I asked Charley at bedtime to sit with me for a while and enjoy the beautiful tree. Charley sat down, reluctantly, I could tell. I was hoping that the beauty of the tree would bring out in us a common feeling, something we could share. But his comments were nothing but platitudes, and I was glad when he went to bed.

A sudden powerful pang of loneliness arose in me. Dagobert would know how to enjoy this thing of beauty, I thought and was overcome by a deep yearning to be with him.

The funeral took place on Monday, a cold and blustery day. Very few people showd up at the funeral parlor's chapel for a memorial service; the Brandon's had no relatives. I saw the apartment manager and his wife, three old ladies from the apartment building, two of Charley's co-workers, and – my heart nearly stopped – there was Dagobert, standing in a far corner as though he was trying to keep out of sight. Our eyes met for a moment, and Dagobert, with a somber expression, nodded toward me. What on earth is he doing here, I wondered while the pastor performed a pious speech about the deceased whom he had not known because Bob had never gone to church. I didn't see Dagobert when we left the chapel.

The group of mourners that made it to the gravesite shrunk to just two beside the Brandons. The coffin, on a rack, lay suspended above green artificial turf that was spread across the dirt piles and the open hole in the ground. No bare earth was visible. I sneered inwardly at the irony of keeping people from seeing and facing the very thing they were undertaking – the burial of a human being. Charley escorted Ida to one of the chairs that were arranged in a row under a canopy. She wore a heavy winter coat but shivered nonetheless. Charley and the twins sat down around her. I stared at the coffin and wondered how many men it had taken to lift and move it. I did not notice Dagobert approaching the grave site until he merged with the few mourners who had braved the cold weather. I looked to Charley who looked at me with a questioning expression.

The pastor said a few hasty words that were whipped away by the icy-cold wind that blew down from the snow-covered mountains to the East and tore at the huge maples and elms that dotted the graveyard. Ida, wrapped in a large blanket, shivered and sniffled and wiped her eyes. There was a three-gun salute by the Veterans of Foreign Wars, the pastor offered his condolences to the family, then everyone disbursed quickly to waiting cars.

Dagobert walked up to Charley and expressed his condolences.

"Do I know you?" Charley asked.

"I'm Dagobert Brandon, your cousin, I believe."

Charley, an only child, did not take in what the stranger had said. He looked to his mother, who looked back at him and shrugged. Ida pressed him to get out of the cold, so Charley turned to head for the car.

"His cousin?" I said, and I noticed that my voice was a little shaky. "You must be mistaken. We don't have any relatives."

"I can assure you that you do," he answered with a warm smile.

"Let's go," said Charley. "It's getting awfully cold."

Charley had not planned for a proper wake. Now I saw an opportunity to learn more about this man. "I tell you what," I said to no one in particular. "Why don't we all go to the Red Apple Café and warm up, and you…" - I was searching for the right address - "you, Mr. Brandon, can tell us what makes you think that you and Charley are cousins, huh?"

"Okay, that sounds great," said Sandy and headed for the car. Judy and Ida followed.

"You have your own car, I suppose?" Charley said to Dagobert.

"Yes. I'll meet you there."

The twins and Ida climbed into the back of the car. The girls began spinning fantasies about long-lost relatives who came back from foreign countries with lots of money and property. Ida tried to squelch their exuberance by pointing out that the Brandons had no relatives, and even if they had, one could never be sure that they were nice people. But the girls were not deterred.

Charley seemed unnerved by the whole thing. "Why did you have to invite him," he grumbled.

"Why not! I want to know what he has to say. I'd love to have some relatives. Maybe you do have some, somewhere. Wouldn't you want to know?"

"I don't need any relatives."

"As if I didn't know," I said with a sigh. "But did it never occur to you that I might like to have some? I grew up with sisters and brothers and cousins, but I never see them. And I do miss them. You never think about that, do you?"

Charley was silent.

The drive to the Red Apple Café was not long. When we entered we saw Dagobert sitting at a large table. He was dressed simply, in dark pants and a plaid flannel shirt with long sleeves. In no way did he let on that he knew me, and I was grateful for it. When we came near he got up to greet us, then everyone sat down, the girls to either side of him so as not to miss anything. After ordering some hot drinks, Charley began by saying, "What is your name again?"

"Dagobert; Dagobert Brandon."

"Strange name. Never heard of it. So you claim to be a cousin of mine. If this is true, how are we related?"

"Your grandfather and my grandfather were brothers. Your grandfather's name is Albert, right?" Charley nodded. "And my grandfather's name is Lester."

"That would make your grandfather an uncle to my father. He never mentioned an uncle on his father's side. Mom, did you ever hear him talking about Brandon relatives?"

"No, he never did."

"Did you ever ask him about his side of the family?" Dagobert queried.

"Not really. Somehow, I got the impression that he hadn't any, so I didn't ask," Ida replied.

I was watching Dagobert closely and noticed the slightest little scorn in his smile, for just a moment. Then it was gone, and the usual serene expression of his eyes returned.

The waitress brought the orders. While she served them, Charley asked, "so, how did you find out about our grandfathers being brothers?"

"It's a rather long story. I bought a piece of property in Northern Idaho. It had an old run-down trailer home on it, some dilapidated sheds, and a lot of all sorts of stuff that the owner must have collected for years. The whole place was overrun with weeds and blackberries, and I couldn't even see what all was there. Once I started clearing the place – and that took a long time – I discovered among the debris an old mailbox with the Brandon name on it. Since my family was the only Brandon family in that area, and the mailbox was not ours, I figured there must have been another Brandon family around. I started researching, and that's how I came across your family. From further research I learned that our grandfathers had a falling out.

Your grandfather left town, and the two never spoke to each other again."

"That's awful!" Judy exclaimed. "To never talk to your brother again! And then they had kids, and the cousins never knew each other. That's terrible. You would never do that, Daddy, would you?"

"My father was an only child," Charley said and turned to Dagobert. "How about your father?"

"My father is dead; he has three younger sisters, though, and they all live in Idaho near the Canadian border." Charley began to fidget on his chair. I nearly laughed to see that the existence of three aunts was making Charley nervous.

"We'll have to go visit them! How many cousins do we have?" Sandy asked eagerly.

"Never mind," Charley said to the girls, obviously irritated. Then, turning to Dagobert, he said, "can you prove all this?"

"Yes I can. I have copies of birth and death certificates. You can look them over any time." Then turning to Sandy, he added "six."

"Six cousins, wow!"

"Where do you live?" Charley asked.

"I tend to go back and forth between here and there."

"So you have property here?"

"Yes, I do."

I realized then that I had never asked Dagobert where he lived or what he did for a living. If he had property nearby, there was a chance I could….. don't be stupid.

After some more chit-chat about family members, and names, and dates, Charley suggested that Dagobert send him copies of the papers. He would look them over. Dagobert agreed. He wrote down our address, then he excused himself and with one more smile at me he left.

I had not said a word the entire time. I had listened intensively, had watched his eyes and his every move and gesture. It seemed to me as though by appearing in my mundane life, he had taken on an equally mundane aspect. His name, Dagobert, which had connected him to my very personal mystery, had quite suddenly taken on a most ordinary connection to the Brandons. I feared the loss of my special relationship with him, a relationship that was not rooted in the mundane side of life.

Talk among the Brandons became more animated after Dagobert left. Charley and his mother speculated about the man's motives; the girls spun plans to meet their relatives; Charley tried to curb their enthusiasm by pointing out that relatives could be undesirable. Ida kept asking what would become of her. And there was talk about moving to a bigger house.

"I need to go home," I suddenly said into the verbal melee.

"That's okay with me," said Charley and stood up.

"No, you don't understand. I need to go home - to Germany."

Charley sat down again. "What brought that on?"

"I need to get away."

"Away from what?"

"I don't know. I just need to go."

"Oh Mom! Can we come too?" the twins nearly yelled as with one voice. I just sat and stared ahead. "Mom? Are you okay?"

"Yes, I'm okay," I said and, as if I had just awakened from a trance, I added. "I'll go right after school is out.

"What about Charley?" Ida said. "Who will look after him when you take a vacation. Charley could use a vacation, too."

"Charley can take a vacation any time he wants to, and if he doesn't take one it's because he doesn't want to. And the girls can cook and do his laundry. They're old enough."

"You should go together. I always waited to go back to New York until the whole family could go."

"But you never made it, did you. And now Bob is dead. Well, I'm not going to let that happen. I'm going in June, right after school is out, after graduation. I'll give myself a graduation present." And, with my voice becoming agitated, I added, "I've gone home only once since I got here. I think I'm entitled to go home again. And if you worry about Charley's well-being then you can cook for him."

"No! We'll do that," said Judy. "We can take care of Daddy, Grandma. You don't need to worry about him."

"Maybe Grandma doesn't want Mom to go to Germany because she never made it to New York," chimed in Sandy with a look of mischief toward Ida.

"That is not a nice thing to say, Sandy," replied Ida indignantly and sniffled.

"I was just teasing, Grandma."

"Who is going to stay with me tonight?"

"I will," Judy said.

The first snowfall happened a few days after Christmas and adorned all things natural and man-made, beautiful and ugly alike. I longed to be outdoors, at the lake where I had met Dagobert. Perhaps he would be there again. But the snow was too deep for driving. I looked in on the dogs, and they seemed excited about the snow. I decided to play with them, and that always meant throwing the ball for Auggie who loved to retrieve it. I had never known anything about dogs, so when I had worked in the yard one day when Auggie was still a pup, I had come across a lot of rocks where I tried to create a flower bed. Not knowing what to do with all the rocks, I had simply thrown them toward the back fence for the time being. And Auggie couldn't wait; each rock that I threw away he faithfully brought back to me and placed it right in front of me, very irritatingly into the very spot that I was working in. At first, I had been annoyed, but eventually I had to laugh about this eager beaver who brought back to me what I hadn't wanted. Then, with a fixed stare at the rock by his feet, and his floppy ears hanging down beside his head, he had stood, his eyes on the rock, waiting for me to pick it up and throw it. Then he had run after it at top speed, kicking up snow or dust, according to the season, that scattered in all directions. Later on, we replaced the rock with a ball and discovered that our dog was a retriever.

While playing with Auggie in the snow, Lassie tried to clean off the snow that accumulated on her legs. The more she chewed it away, though, the wetter her legs became and the more snow they attracted until large globs of white ice dangled on her black legs and weighed her down. Just like people, I thought; while one is able to enjoy the season, the other only sees problems

A few days later high school and college resumed. I arrived early and went straightway to the cafeteria in hopes of meeting Dagobert. But I was disappointed; Dagobert was not there. I waited till my class started, and after every class I came for a brief look around, but I did not find him. After my last class was over I waited a long time, staring out the window and wondering what might have happened to him, or to us. I began to realize that I had never considered that there was more to the man than what I had seen in his eyes, that he had a life, a family perhaps, a job, responsibilities, perhaps even passions that did not include me. But all that had found no place in my dreams. I had been dreaming about an idol, not a human being. Discovering it made me feel quite foolish.

With a deep sigh I got up and left.

It was going to be a long flight from the west coast of the United States to Europe. I sat back in my seat and closed my eyes to more fully experience the best part of the flight - take-off. I loved that feeling of power that permeates the entire plane as the engines rev up, the plane begins to roll down the runway, speeds up, shaking and vibrating as if straining against a force that would hold it back, faster and faster till the wheels come off the ground and the giant bird is in flight.

I did not get a window seat, so after the plane had taken off and the world had vanished in puffs of mist there was nothing for me to do but think. My thoughts traveled unrestricted across time and space as one dimension. The change from the ordinary environment of home to the unusual environment of air travel brought out a different set of memories from those that I lived with every day. Venusbrunn came to mind, the boarding school with its beautiful little park and the gate where I had met with Willi a few times. I wiggled around in my seat to find a long-lasting comfortable position. Then I closed my eyes to recall Willi's face. But I couldn't. It was more than twenty-five years since then. And I had lost the locket that held pictures of him and me. In teeny-tiny script he had written on a tiny card: reach out with your mind and you will find me. His mother had given it to me on my last day at Venusbrunn when I came to see him. But Willi had died.

The plane hummed and cruised and lulled me to sleep. A nudge from the passenger in the seat beside mine brought me back to Flight Nr.117 to Frankfurt on Main, Germany. The hostess was bringing a meal, and I loved eating out. I didn't care much for cooking, never had, and I didn't mind admitting it. It was a lot of work for something that disappeared in just minutes. And since I didn't care for it, planning a meal was a chore. Many times I just threw something together. Then, after having eaten a lot of these unplanned thrown-together meals I got tired of my own cooking. Then I'd pull out a cook book, search out a delicious-to-read receipt and cook a proper meal. More often than not, though, it didn't turn out right, which discouraged me from trying out further new meals. And so, I'd be back to my unplanned thrown-together meals. - My neighbor grumbled about the food, but I liked it. Then I went back to thinking.

Since old man Brandon's death Ida had bugged us about moving to a bigger house so she could live with us. Charley had managed to keep her where she was, but he was beginning to tire of her incessant talking about it – how very much like Charley - and I had come to fear that another move would be forced on me. Worse, I feared that once again I would give in simply because I got tired of Charley's unending pressure tactics. Then again, my going to school had begun to make him understand a few things, like listening when I had a problem, or letting me have my way in a few things, or that I was not afraid to live alone if he annoyed me enough. Just how close he came, he would probably never know. Before I left on this trip I had told him that if he loved me, truly loved me, he would not make me move again. I didn't tell him that if he disregarded my wish and force another move on me, our marriage would be over. I wanted to give him a chance to do it my way without an ultimatum. I had left with the understanding that he would try to find other means to satisfy his mother.

After the second meal, and once the hostesses had cleared the isles, I went to the restroom and did a few stretches in the small corridor by the galley kitchen. There was nothing to be seen through the windows. The plane was packed with people, there were no empty seats on which I might have stretched out. So while I was walking up and down I did some people watching: trying to guess passengers' reasons for the flight, what males and females were, perhaps, couples or, perhaps, not, what might be their final destination. Then I went back to my seat, made myself as comfortable as possible and let the hum of the engines and the sound of soft voices take over again.

Dagobert Brandon came to mind. I was still puzzled by his behavior and had never seen him again. Habit had made me look up and around the college cafeteria every time I had entered, but it was just habit. And he was never there. I had resigned myself to the fact that this relationship – what there had been of it - had run its course, which had set me free to apply myself totally to my studies, and the result had been excellent grades.

And one Dagobert led to another - the historical one of my obsession. Dagobert II was a member of the Merowingian family dynasty that ruled from the fifth to eighth centuries in what was then Gaul and is today France. It was a Frankish kingdom that was regarded not so much as a state but as a property, and it was considered natural that it should be divided on the death of a king among his sons. This situation had promoted incessant fighting and murder among sons, grandsons, wives and mothers who each sought to consolidate their rule over the total property.

Dagobert's father died early, and his political rivals could be expected to get rid of the young Dagobert II. To save him, the Bishop of Poitiers took the child for its safety to live with a Scottish royal family. This much history I had been able to glean from a very short supply of available information. Many years later, Dagobert's enemies arranged for a hunting trip during which Dagobert II was murdered in the forest. And that story had been on my mind all the years since 6th grade when we had read the book "Dagobert's Krone" in class.

When I reached Hanfurt I would search for that book, the book that had brought him into my life. My brother Walter would surely help me find it on the Internet. The computer that Charley had bought for a Christmas present stood on a small table in a corner of the dining room. It had nearly overwhelmed the girls with joy to receive it, and it had definitely helped to improve the somber mood following grandpa's death. I had not had time to do anything other than learn the use of the word processor so I could do my class work. The presence of this new gadget had caused the girls to quarrel some at first, each one trying to be first or have equal time at the machine. It had been that way with their brand new driver licenses. But once they had come up with a time plan that worked out well for them peace reigned again. And they learned the use of it quickly. Must be due to a younger mind, I thought, a mind that is still flexible because it does not yet have formed the many ruts that habitual thinking patterns create in the brain over a lifetime, into which, then, all thinking falls, the way vehicles keep falling into the mud ruts on a dirt road.

The sky was lead gray on arrival in Frankfurt early morning. It didn't surprise me; it seemed to be the standard for this city that is situated on the river Main not far from its confluence with the river Rhein. The airport has a direct connection to Frankfurt's main railroad station, and from there, a fast train took me to Hanfurt in little more than an hour.

I hadn't told anyone that I was coming because I wanted to have some fun with them, watching their faces at the sight of me. It would start with a look of dull confusion that would turn to disbelief, then recognition, followed by astonishment at my sudden appearance and then, hopefully, joy to see me. All this would take just a few seconds.

It was late morning when I arrived in Hanfurt. I stopped outside the station building to take in the sight of Bahnhofstrasse that sloped straight ahead, past my family home to the heart of the city. It had been a good eighteen hours from getting up in the US till arriving in Hanfurt. My head was in a fog from lack of sleep, and looking around at the people who were rushing by, not taking note of me as though I were invisible, felt like being in the twilight zone.

I picked up my heavy luggage and drudged down the street; it was only two blocks to the four-floor family house with the retail store on the street level. I placed my luggage in a corner of the family store and explained to the clerks – there were no familiar faces among them - who I was, and asked them not to reveal to the boss that he had company from America.

Walter used the same office that Father had used on the second floor of the building. I didn't knock but entered very quietly. I was lucky; he was sitting at his desk, looking over some papers, and he hadn't heard me coming in. I could see that his thick coarse hair was getting thin around the crown and that it had already turned quite a bit gray. Just like Father, I thought. I had never known him but with a meager gray hair wreath around his bald crown. We used to think it funny that he would take a comb to what little hair was left to him.

"Hello, Wally!" I said and watched for the expected expressions. I was not disappointed. It was hilarious to watch the changing emotions spread so clearly over his face. Then, with a sheepish grin, like father's, he got up and came to me and we shook hands. Oh, what the heck, I thought and hugged him instead. It was something that I had learned from Charley and I was glad that he had taught me.

"You feel like an ironing board."

"Well…," he said and grinned self-consciously. And just then I discovered that this characteristic grin of Fathers and his, with the corners of the mouth turned down instead of up as in a smile, expressed something I had never understood before. It was like an urge to smile in response to a feeling of happiness or pleasure, but inhibition, caused by a fear of revealing something personal, held him back. And the only thing that Walter could have revealed at that moment was a show of true feelings. He preferred shaking hands because it maintains distance, while hugs feel intrusive. How very sad.

"I'm not…" Walter started.

"I know, I know. You're not used to hugs. Neither was I. But it's something that Charley taught me, and I'm glad. So, how are you doing old man?"

"I'm fine, but how come you didn't let me know that you were coming?"

"I wanted to surprise you," I said and looked him closely in the eyes because I knew he would be so cute, squirming and grinning with self-consciousness. And he did.

"That's obvious. But my place is a mess."

"Oh, don't worry about it. I won't organize your precious mess. I just need a bed and very little else. Or are you afraid to let me see your bachelor pad?"

"Some bachelor pad!" he said with a short laugh. "But I think you'll like the changes I made after Mother died. Come on, let's go upstairs. You're probably hungry? It's almost lunch time anyway."

"Would you go downstairs first and pick up my suitcase? I left it there for the guys to watch."

"Okay, you go ahead."

I walked up to the third floor landing and looked out over the loading yard and the two fronts of the L-shaped warehouse complex that was part of the family property. Straight across was the window that I could see from our playroom. When Mother had been pregnant with number eight, the story had gone around that the stork will bring a girl if white sugar is placed on the outside window sill, for the stork to find and take, but will bring a boy if brown sugar is placed there. I had had my doubts. And in order to check the validity of that story and perhaps outsmart the stork, I had placed sugar on the sill of the warehouse window. And sure enough, the stork had never found it.

I looked up to the flat roof that had been our playground. The cyclone fence that surrounded it was still in place, and the intermittent tall poles with hooks at the upper end to support clothes lines were there. It was always nice up there on a sunny spring day, and I had never minded hanging laundry. There had been sun chairs for our use and a play house built by some of the employees who were trained carpenters. We had even spent a hot summer night once on cots and feather beds for a cover. Mother had insisted that the featherbeds were needed against the morning chill. I hadn't believed it but learned that she was right.

I went to the third floor and to the next landing from which I had an even better view including more sky. On that window sill I had often paused to look at the sky or listen to a bird that, I later learned, was of the same species as the American Robin and sounded very much like it. On quiet summer weekend afternoons, when all businesses including ours had shut down, that bird song had played up an atmosphere of sheer tranquility. Since then, every time I hear a Robin, I am transferred back to that window, and I feel that same sense of tranquility.

Walter had entered the apartment and I followed him. The long corridor had a new carpet and new wallpaper. The once painted doors from the corridor to the rooms had been replaced with doors in natural wood tones. I hung up my coat on the hallstand and followed Walter to the kitchen. It had changed a lot. It had the latest in kitchen furniture and kitchen gadgets. Gone was the big old wood and coal fired stove that mother had used for many years. And for canning tons of fruit and vegetables it had been the only way to work. Walter had created a little sitting area instead.

"I like what you did here," I said and sat down on the pretty little chair, one of a couple that matched a small square table that was just right for a single person's breakfast. It made me ask, "still no wedding in sight, huh?"

"Nope."

"Do you mind my asking personal questions?"

"Well, just not too personal, please."

"Just let me know if I'm going too far. Okay, why haven't you married? Aren't there enough women around?"

"I tell you what," he said. "It's lunchtime, and I have some left-over casserole from last night. My housekeeper comes three times a week and cooks something to last a couple of days. Want some?"

I couldn't help but laugh. "Okay, I get the message. As to the food, let me see what it is."

Walter pulled a bowl out of the refrigerator and removed the lid. I sniffed it, and since it smelled good I agreed. Walter put the bowl in the microwave oven to warm up the food. Meanwhile, I went to the bathroom, which also had been redone with the most modern and luxurious bath fixtures I had ever seen. The six foot very deep bathtub that had begun to lose its enamel from decades of cleaning and scrubbing had been replaced by a new one of equal size. The bathroom water heater that had been fired with wood and coal had given way to a central water heating system. And the toilet had also been replaced with a modern one of American design. The aqua tiles of the walls, and the black and white tiles of the floor had been replaced with new tiling of sophisticated colors and design. I freshened up a bit, then went back to the kitchen where the food was ready to eat.

"Well, what do you think of my bathroom?"

"It's gorgeous.. And that big tub of yours – I'd like to have one just like it. Did you design the remodel or did you get professional help?"

"No, I did it pretty much on my own. Paula and Hildi came and looked from time to time and made suggestions, and some of their ideas were pretty useful. But other than that – it's my work." Walter was obviously pleased with himself.

"Do me a favor, Walter. Call the others and let them know I'm here. Perhaps we could all get together somewhere, maybe outdoors since the weather is so nice, for coffee, or lunch, whatever."

"Sure, be glad to. But I think that one or the other of the boys is on vacation. I know that Hildi is at home, and Paula – well, you can see her at the shop."

We talked while we ate. I had a lot of questions, and Walter filled me in on many little family details that never manage to get into a letter but are so very helpful for better or more clearly understanding what is being told. When we were done eating, he excused himself and went back to his office but not before showing me where I could sleep. He had bought an attractive bedstead for his guest-room. My simple post-war two-by-four platform bed, built and padded by carpenters was gone. I unpacked my luggage, and then, placing my crossed arms on the deep windowsill for comfort, I watched the German world go by down below.

It had changed a lot. The villa with its garden that once stood across from our building, had been razed to make room for a parking garage whose purpose was cleverly hidden by a façade of small shops, cafes and offices. The tennis court with its clubhouse beside the villa had been the first thing to go. Traffic had increased tremendously. One-way streets necessitated ridiculous detours. People hurried, hurried, hurried in every direction. The big linden trees that once graced Bahnhofstrasse along the Northwest side of our house had died from winter ice and salt; the replacements were small. And the great chestnut trees on Lindenstrasse that bordered our house on the southwest had been removed with a strip of sidewalk to make room for cars.

I went downstairs. The sun was shining now, and I walked in the direction of the city castle. On the way, I came by the state library and went inside to see if the book about Dagobert could be located. All I knew was the title, neither author nor anything else. To my disappointment, it was not known there. But the librarian suggested that I check out a local bookstore that carried books out of print. I took down the address and continued on to the city castle grounds, a park with a pond and many walkways, shrubs and ancient trees, the sight of which conjured up countless memories of Leon and Charley.

I walked through it and came out opposite the baroque cathedral. Beyond and to the left lay the old town where the bookstore was located. I found it easily enough, but the book I wanted was not available. The proprietor knew the book I was looking for, but he was sorry not to carry it anymore. To make sure, he went on the internet and explored opportunities there. But it was no use.

Deep in thought I left that little shop. Outside, looking around in all directions, I picked a little street that I had never known. I walked on, getting farther and farther away from city center. Suddenly, the row of houses on my right ended but continued farther back from the sidewalk. The little square that was thus formed was paved with cobblestones, and in the center of the square stood a tall linden tree in the embrace of a circular wooden bench. Good God, I thought, it's the setting for folk songs about lovers' sad farewells.

Directly behind the tree was a house with stone steps that led to the entrance of a small inn. "The Crown" said a sign above the entry. Dagobert's Crown was the title of my coveted book. Was it an omen? To the right and left of the inn a few old houses had settled into each other long ago. It was an enchanting place, quiet, peaceful, far from city noise, as if the world had forgotten it and two wars had never noticed it. As I looked closer at the other houses I noticed a shop sign above one door. It was facing away from me, so I walked closer to see what it said. To my surprise, it was a bookshop. The door was locked. Peeking through the window with my hands against the glass to block out glare revealed only books. But a sign in the window named the store hours. I would be back.

I walked back the way I had come, or so I thought. But somehow, I ended up in a crowded shopping area. The summer heat reflecting off the dark pavement had sapped my strength. When I saw the café that Ulla and I used to frequent I went inside. The front of it was more like a bakery, where I picked out the pastry and ordered coffee; a waitress then brought it to me in the sitting area. I took my time, watching the customers coming and going, always with a thought in the back of my mind that I might see someone I knew. Several older ladies, each one on her own table, were drinking coffee - probably taking a break from shopping.

On the way home I came by my parish church, and I went inside. As always in summer, the change in temperature from the street to that of the church was very abrupt and definitely refreshing on a hot day. I sat down on one of the very heavy old wooden benches with their infinitely marked up surfaces, and with my eyes I checked out all the little details I used to study as a child during boring sermons – the pattern of the marble columns, the naked little cherubs of painted pictures who always had a bit of cloth between their legs, the number of candles and flower vases on the altar. Leon and I had often sat together in a church to think, to rest, to talk. We even exchanged rings when we became engaged.

In thinking about Leon, I wondered what our marriage would have been like. Leon had taught me, not in words but in actions, how a man should treat a woman. Our lives would probably have been filled with work, and children, and saving money for our own little house and car. My parents would have eventually accepted but not treasured him. Would we have fought and quarreled like most people? I could not imagine it. Would our romance have died the way it did in so many marriages? My romance with Charley had died eventually. Silently and unnoticed it had vanished over time. Perhaps that was the way of all romances. It might even be a good thing because constant emotional and sexual arousal would be hardly bearable over time. Maybe a good relationship is one that grows to be comfortable and steadfast over the years, when two people have come to know each other well, don't try to change the partner but accept each other's viewpoints and habits readily and without complaints. Throughout my married years with Charley I sometimes recalled the night Leon and I made love for the first and only time. Charley had never measured up. And I wondered if I had been fair to Charley to compare him to Leon. Perhaps I should just be grateful for having had Leon in my life. If I hadn't known him I wouldn't know what I was missing in Charley's love-making, and I wouldn't yearn for that which I could no longer have. I might be content, but would I be happy? I would never know.

When people started coming into the church, and someone busied himself at the altar with lighting of candles, I realized that Wednesday evening mass would soon begin. I decided to stay.

Walter told me later that evening of the plans he had made for the family gathering on the following Sunday afternoon at a place that we all knew. Just nine miles from Hanfurt is a pretty little grassy valley, surrounded by woods, where a small church for pilgrims had been built during the fourteenth century. Like anything that has survived that long, the church had undergone many changes, had many owners, had survived wars, neglect and renovations. A country inn had established itself nearby, and the whole area had become a favorite outing for the people of Hanfurt, hikers or not. I was looking forward to it.

Next day, I went to the mysterious little bookshop. That was the plan, anyway. I couldn't find it, though. No matter what I tried, I could not find the way to it. There were moments when I thought I might have dreamed the whole thing, that I had never really seen it. Tired of walking and searching, I went back to Walter and asked him about it. He had no knowledge of such a shop. Just how often does he buy books, I wondered. Walter was not much of a reader. Then I asked him to search the Internet for me. He said he would.

Later that day, still puzzled about the bookshop and wanting to meditate I climbed up Bishops Hill that is crowned with a Franciscan monastery and a beautiful baroque church. Leon and I had gone there several times; it was a great place to rest from a long walk. And after the climb on a hot summer afternoon it was great to cool off in the church - until I began to feel cold in my summer dress. Bishops Hill connects with a slightly larger hill that has a wilder appearance, is full of big old trees and shrubs, underbrush and walkways. Many little groves and grottos lend themselves well to meditation. I found my favorite bench, sat down and closed my eyes. A slight breeze wafted through the treetops, and the rustling of the leaves and the gentle murmur in the evergreen trees was the perfect background sound for meditation.

As so often, Dagobert was very much on my mind. I called his name, spoke it out loud and concentrated on it. It did not take long for me to feel a presence. It sent shivers down my spine. In my mind, I reached out to it, and at the same time the words "come to me" escaped me. The presence I felt came to me, I reached out to it and we embraced. And in that embrace, the presence melted into me and I knew that Dagobert and I were one and the same spirit.

Tears of joy and exhilaration rose in my eyes as the magnitude of this revelation began to set in. It gripped me so thoroughly that I sat quietly for a long time, thunderstruck at knowing that all these years that I was thinking of Dagobert I was actually creating a connection to one of my previous lives. Then I realized that the sadness I had so often felt during meditation had passed between us during our embrace.

I was so preoccupied with this event that, later that evening, Walter asked if anything was wrong. I could only smile. Things could have been no more right. I didn't speak about it though. Society had imparted to me certain values, and an experience such as mine was considered to belong in the realm of psychosis. But I had been touched by this attitude enough to ask myself many times if what I had experienced was really true or just a figment of my imagination. But I knew it was true; I knew it inside myself. How does one convince someone of a truth that is known only inside oneself? It's not possible. I remembered a certain professor who had said more than once that he never teaches us anything we don't already know. It sounded absurd at the time, but I knew now just how right he had been.

Walter went to his Stammtisch, a kind of weekly round-table gathering place in a Gasthaus for his group of buddies. "Could you ask your beer buddies if they know that book shop I couldn't find again," I asked him. "It's right near that little Gasthaus, called Krone."

"Why don't you come with me and ask them yourselves. You know some of the guys, and they sometimes ask about you."

"Ahhh...I don't think so. I can't see myself spending an entire evening among smokers and drinkers."

"You make us sound pretty bad," Walter replied with a frown.

"Well - whatever you're used to. Charley doesn't smoke, and I don't like those stinking halls anymore. Of course he loves his beer, too. But, no thanks."

"How about Friday – you want to come bowling with me and the group?"

"Sure, I'd like that." But I knew that the environment there would be no different. The group would be talking loudly, drink plenty of beer and hard liqueur and smoke lots of cigarettes. It would create a kind of visual and auditory fog that would actually keep out the uninitiated, namely me. I was very glad that Charley didn't smoke. As Walter walked out of the apartment I called after him, "don't forget to ask them."

With Walter gone out, I decided to meditate again; perhaps I would learn more. Walter had a wonderfully comfortable recliner that was perfect for meditation. I turned on the radio and found a station with soothing music. Then I sat down, I closed my eyes and visualized myself near a stairway that leads down into a garden. I went down those steps, walked through the flower beds that stretched along both sides of the path. It was a beautiful sight. At the end of the path was another set of steps that led further down into another flower garden. After walking through it, another set of steps led me even further down into a meadow that bordered a castle wall. I followed a path to the left as it led along the castle wall, and I came to a tower with an open door. The opening was pitch black and felt ominous. I shrank from it yet felt the urge to step inside where I saw a circular stairway. I began to climb it, higher and higher. I came to an opening on the side that seemed to lead into the main part of the castle. I felt that I should keep going. Finally, I made it to the top. I stepped out onto the platform, into sunshine, and walked toward the battlements. There, I was prompted to look down, and when I did, I saw the body of a small child on the ground below. And suddenly, I knew that this child was mine and was Dagobert's, and that its death was the cause of all the sadness that connected us.

I came around with tears running down my face. Awe and sadness in turn gave me shivers and goosebumps. I sat for a long time thinking, analyzing, trying to digest what I had just learned. I've got to find that book, I thought. This book, Dagoberts Krone, had initiated me into long years of searching, of soulsearching, of reaching out to my High Self. It had become the impetus for all the learning that Spirit in its physical form is meant to accomplish on this earth during many life times, wearing many garments, living many roles. Would the book confirm what I had just learned? It didn't matter. I wanted to hold this treasure in my hands. Fear that I might not find it caused me a restless night.

"Come on! Let's get going," Walter called for me Saturday afternoon. I was in the bathroom fixing my hair, and I wanted it to be just right. But, as so often, every one of my so-called permanent curls – which, of course, they never were - had its own idea about which way to lie, and the two cowlicks on the back of my head seemed more contrary than ever.

"Oh what the heck!" I left my contrary head to itself and went out. We went downstairs, climbed into his pewter gray Mercedes and headed for our meeting place. We were quiet. I could feel more than see Walter looking me over from the side. Then he said, "what's that grin on your face for? You look different."

At first, I wasn't sure what to tell him. Then I said, "Just how do I look?"

"Oh, I don't know – just different – happy maybe."

"Happy, huh? Well, I should be. I had a fantastic experience."

"What qualifies as a fantastic experience?"

"I don't think you want to know."

"No, tell me."

"Well, I had this experience while meditating," I figured it couldn't hurt to give a little hint just to see if, by chance, he had developed an interest in the metaphysical realm.

"Oh, - you're right, I don't want to know," he said with a short laugh. "But, listen," he continued. You know that Paula is going through a divorce, right?"

"What? - I don't know that at all!"

"Well, you know it now. It's a really messy affair regarding the property settlement. Father thought he was being smart when he advised Werner and her about how they should handle their tax set-up, because of the shop. It might have been okay, or maybe even financially rewarding while they were married, but now that they want to separate, it looks like Paula has to fight for every little bit of property, even her own stuff that she brought into the marriage."

"So she's finally dumping the jerk. I wonder what took her so long. And of course it never occurred to Father that any one of us might get divorced some day."

"You sound as though you might consider it yourself," Walter asked with a sideways glance.

"Well, let's just say we had our difficulties. Is there anything else I should know before we get there?"

"Hans is coming with his wife and children. Markus and his wife are coming, but Matthias is on vacation. His marriage doesn't look so good either. He's got a sweet wife, but he doesn't treat her right. And Hildi, of course, is coming."

Ten minutes later we arrived at the café across from that little old church that had seen so many centuries pass by. We walked over to the open seating area, and the first one I saw was Hildi. She spotted me at the same moment, got up and came over to me. Overjoyed, we hugged each other the way we had always done. And, as she had always done, she looked me over very carefully while I stood still as a statue. Then she smiled, satisfied. She had her hair put up in a bun on the back of her head, and her face and body had become a little fuller. She wore very little make-up, and she wore a bright flowery sundress.

Before I could comment on her pretty womanly appearance Hans and Markus had come around to hug me, or rather, shake hands with me.

"Hey, you guys!" is all I could get out before Paula came upon the scene and hugged me, and I hugged her. A quick look at her face showed me that it was still smooth as a baby's behind. Not a trace of any hardship could I see in it. You lucky dog, I thought. She drew a young woman near and asked, "do you recognize Matty?" and before I could answer she motioned a young man over to us and asked, "and Gustav?"

"Oh Mom! You know I hate that name," he complained with a grimace, and turning to me, he added, "I call myself "Usta, aunt Fanny." He and Matty had grown into handsome young people.

"You should have brought your twins, it would have been such fun," Matty said

"I would have loved to do that, but we just can't afford it. But how about you visiting us? I think your Dad makes a lot more money than my Charley."

"We'll have to work on him," Matty said enthusiastically.

Hans, the teacher, then introduced his wife, Hannelore who was also a teacher, and their three boys. And Markus, the Engineer presented his wife, Anita, a beautiful woman with black hair, an olive complexion, and large dark eyes that betrayed a fiery temperament. I knew, of course, that he had found her on one of his business trips to Egypt, and I wondered how she had adjusted to the German "ironing boards."

"Come on, everybody, sit down. Coffee is ready," Hildi called, and with a large coffee pot she went around the table filling the cups that stood ready. My eyes ogled the pastry platters. I sat down with Paula and she told me the sad ugly story of Werner's escapades, and how his once rude behavior had become abusive over the years. She was in love with someone else and hoped to get out of her marriage with at least that which she had brought into the union. Of course, being Catholic added its own set of problems to her predicament.

"How come you never told me in your letters?" I asked.

"You know that I don't have much time for writing," she answered. "And then when I did write, I just didn't feel like telling all this ugly stuff."

"You didn't write often but you surely wrote great letters. They were always so full of interesting details. Some people write letters that say absolutely nothing."

I kept changing places at the long table in order to have a visit with every one of my siblings. I could see from the way Hans treated his boys that he had become a good father. I liked to think that I had a little something to do with it, and it made me feel proud. Father and Mother certainly had not been a good example of how parents ought to treat their children. It must have been very frustrating for them to try to rear us with commands and seeing all the while that it didn't work. Hans' hairline had receded a little, his slender body had spread out into a tall manly figure. He treated his wife well, and she seemed to be a warm and caring person. And Markus, the engineer, had also followed his inclination. It had taken a long time for Father to accept the fact that none of his sons would follow in his brother John's footsteps as an Army officer. And what about Matthias, I asked. He had married at only twenty-one years of age, and before he had made a career for himself. His wife was even younger and she had only an eighth grade education. They had three children in quick succession, did not keep in touch with the others and joined few family gatherings. It made me sad to hear it. I would try to visit him.

When we got tired of sitting we went to the little church. It was open, and we had a chance to view the results of the latest restoration. Then we walked along the woods, changing conversation partners from time to time. Hans' three boys usually ran ahead. A nearby farm's horse was grazing in a pasture and Paula reminded me of another time when we had hiked to this place. We had found a horse idling in the meadow then, too. With great expectations, my inner cowboy had prompted me to climb the horse. But the horse had known nothing of my great expectations. It simply grazed and walked slowly down the sloping pasture, and not having anything to hold on to I promptly slid down over the horse's neck and head and – thud, into the meadow.

Then Hildi came around and walked with me for a stretch. She had become a pediatric nurse but had no children of her own. Her husband, a medical doctor, was on duty at the hospital that afternoon. Hildi had found a mentor who taught her how to control and develop her spiritual gifts. It had given her a wonderful advantage in dealing with sick children – she could always tell if something other than the diagnosed problem was bothering a child. Her reputation was known by other hospitals as well, and she was often sought out for her advice. She was delighted when I told her of my encounter with Dagobert, the physical being of my previous life. It was so good to converse with such an open and accepting spirit.

"How about Walter," I asked.

"I don't think he'll ever marry. It's as if he doesn't want to grow up and have any more responsibilities than what he already has. He's got plenty of that as a business owner, and I guess that's enough for him. He wants to be able to take two vacations a year, and he loves his freedom to come and go as he pleases. And who can blame him since he has no children. And then there are the choir and the bowling group, the gun club and the hiking club, and let's not forget the Stammtisch. So, he's got plenty of people around him, and none of them tie him down, see? But what about you? I remember a sour note in one of your last letters. And you actually don't write so much anymore. What's up?"

"I did go through a bad period with Charley. But studying at the college did me a lot of good, not just the studying, but meeting other people. I'd been pretty isolated for years. I was so dumb – well, not really dumb but inexperienced, and Charley took advantage of it. I came close to divorcing him."

"It's that bad, huh?"

"You bet. Eventually, he did try harder to consider my feelings. So now, I'm just waiting to see what'll happen when I get back. I figure that if he really loves me he won't make me move again – he thought we should so that Ida could live with us, which is what she wants but I don't. So, if he still insists, it's over. I just won't do it. Even if I do end up lonely and miserable. But I would still have the girls, and they're a real joy. I never forgot just how lonely and miserable I was before I met Leon. That's probably what kept me from divorcing Charley at the first impulse." Hildi put her arm in mine and we walked on like that. "But you know, discovering that the Spirit which inhabited Dagobert inhabits me now – it still awes me – is such a profound thing that it seems to minimize whatever little problems I think I have. I mean, we must be going through all sorts of things in the course of so many life times, good and bad, and that losing Leon is just one of those, but it's certainly not the end of life. Maybe that's why we don't remember everything from the past. It would kill us to know all the dreadful things we've gone through – and maybe even committed."

"When I drive alongside a river, and there's no or not much of a shoulder, I can easily panic for fear of losing control and drowning in the river," Hildi said with a shudder. "I must have drowned in a previous life."

"Did you discover any of your past lives?"

"No, not exactly. Everybody's path is a little different – unique for everyone. It's like a specialized course of instruction created just for each one of us."

"That's a great though! But tell me, what does your husband think about these things?"

"Not much," she answered with a short laugh. "You'd think I would marry someone who is more like me. Oh, nature is very tricky; it makes us fall in love with people who need us to help them grow - and for them to help us grow, why not. Nobody's perfect. Robert, being a medical doctor and scientist, sees life different from me. So I have to help him, slowly but carefully, understand that medical science doesn't know much about real life. And he's open to it – to a degree." After a while she asked," what are you going to do with your education?"

"I don't know yet. I might go on for a BA degree, maybe not. The girls will be going to College, and they should come first. So, maybe I better find a job and earn some money first – we'll see. I wouldn't mind a sense of independence for a change. Maybe I'd meet other women my age, make some friends. That would be nice, too."

Before we said good-bye Paula invited me for a drive in the country, including a visit to the cemetery on the way. Hans and his wife would have Walter and me over for dinner, and Hildi invited me to see the city castle's reception hall that had undergone careful renovation with original materials. And we'd have dinner some night when her husband, the doctor, could be counted on being at home. Markus and his wife offered to take me on a tour of historical architectural jewels along Germany's Romantic Road, and I was delighted at the prospect. I would not be bored.

I couldn't wait for Monday to roll around so that I could look for the little bookshop again. Walter had been no help, and none of my siblings knew anything of it. I started out the way I had done the first time, through the castle gardens across the street and down the left side of the cathedral, not really searching for it but, like being blind, allowing memory to guide me. And indeed, I found it again. It was open this time and I went right in. Opening the door stirred a bell, and a little old man appeared from around a bookcase. He was short and hunched over, his gray hair hanging into his face and nearly obliterating his spectacles. He looked up at me and smiled, saying "good morning. What can I do four you, young lady?"

"I'm looking for a book I knew a long time ago. All I remember is the title, Dagobert's Krone. I know nothing else about it, not even the author."

He nodded with a smile of recognition, as if he had known that I would ask for it. It was quite eerie. He turned and disappeared in the dark, dusty abyss of bookshelves, and after a little while he reappeared with a book in his hand. I could hardly believe my eyes. There it was: the book about Dagobert's life and death that I had hoped to find again for such a long time. I grabbed it eagerly. The little man smiled and mentioned the price. I gladly paid, said good-bye and left.

Once outside, I couldn't wait. I sat down on the bench under the linden tree and began to read. The story was called "A King's Legend." A few people came and went to and from the inn, a car pulled up and left again. The sun shone through the leafy canopy and threw lacy shadows on the cobblestones. As eager as I was to devour the book on the spot, I decided to take it slowly, not rush through it and then forget most of what I read. The otherworldly feel of this idyllic place wanted me to stay and enjoy it, and I gave in. Meanwhile, the book lay in my lap like a treasure that would always be mine now. No more searching and wondering about it. I had the real thing, and I would explore it privately, without distractions, and in no hurry.

After a while, with the book in my bag and probably a very contented smile on my face I felt free to give my attention totally to my explorations. I wanted to see all the big and little corners and streets and places of Hanfurt that I had never really known because errands imposed by Mother had always required hurry. I found myself walking where I had been happy with Charley. There was the bridge over the Hanfurt river where we met for our first date – far from home so that there was no danger of being seen by family members. But just as we had come together that day, my parents had driven by in Father's baby blue Volkwagen. Quite certain that they had seen me, and worried about the consequences, I had thought it best to tell nonchalantly that I had taken an American GI on a tour of

Hanfurt. I could have kicked myself when I found out that they had not seen me, and that I had given away freely what I would have treasured solely for myself.

I could never bring Charley home. Father held a grudge against Americans for the occupation, for their wasteful use of electricity, which Germans had to pay for; for make-up and chewing gum, casual behavior, addressing girls with "hi, baby!" and sitting crosswise on the window sills of the ground level café across the street, which my younger brother Hans promptly copied in our third floor living room window. German windows had no screens but two wings that opened wide.

And there was that little restaurant where we often had dinner. Charley fed me well; he thought I was too thin. Wiener Schnitzel with salt potatoes and salad was our favorite. Of course Charley always added "Brot und Butter, bitte," (bread and butter please.) Charley liked his beer, but he didn't want me to drink it, so I always ordered apple juice. I knew that he wanted to keep me safe and I liked that. One sunny Sunday afternoon he had actually brought me a pint of ice cream from the army base and then hurried to our meeting place to give it to me. To my delight, it was still eatable with a spoon instead of drinkable from the carton.

The back courtyard of the city castle with its fountain was one of our meeting places. One time, Charley had come early because he wanted to hide there; passes had been revoked after he had received his, and MPs where driving about, collecting stray GIs. They did not find Charley.

I went through the parks, sought out every spot where we had been and sat down on our favorite bench, the one that was slightly hidden by overhanging trees and shrubbery. I was glad to see that it was still there, even with a fresh coat of paint. It had been hard to find privacy in public places, but we had found some. It was on that bench that Charley had kissed me for the first time. And I noticed that the memory of it made me smile.

When I left Hanfurt, Hildi, Walter, and Paula saw me off. I couldn't help but shed a few tears; I had always missed my siblings for Charley had such a tiny family. But some day, the girls would get married and I would add their husbands and families to my own. And they would most likely have children who would increase my family even more. We would have great times and lots of fun, babies and children to hug and teach and watch growing up. Charley loved little children; he would take them fishing in the river and horseback-riding in the mountains.

I wondered how he had handled the matter of Ida.

Aboard the plane, I pulled out the book to read the last few pages, describing how one of Dagobert's enemies, not open but secret, lured him to a hermitage in the woods. On the way they came to a newly woven bridge of wood and branches that led across a trench. As he led his horse across, it seemed to be strong enough, but suddenly it collapsed, sending him and his horse into the depth. He came to lie on top of the horse, and once he had collected himself he looked up to see the hatefully sneering face of his companion. Then something hit him hard on the head and he lost consciousness. In his last moments Sigibert, his little boy and heir to the crown, appeared to him in spiritual form. With unspeakable pain Dagobert realized that his son had already been killed.

Very little history of the lives of the Merowingian kings has come down to us. The author of this book, Gertrud Zender, wrote that the son of Dagobert II, Sigibert, had been murdered in his little bed. She could not have known that he had been thrown from the tower. But I knew it. And I knew now why I felt drawn to Scotland, and especially Ireland where Dagobert had spent the happiest years of his life in a peaceful convent among a group of learned monks. Perhaps that is why I had felt happily at home in the convent of Venusbrunn while all the other girls complained about being caged and not having access to radios or friends. And perhaps it is the reason why I love the northern countries with their rugged landscapes and rough climates. Like finding the roots of one's human existence, I discovered that it is no less rewarding or important to discover the roots of one's spiritual being. Since the days of my youth, Spirit had been calling to me through countless seemingly accidental happenings, ever patiently waiting for me to hear and respond to it. It was an exhilarating journey of discovery that has not ended.

Additional books by Rita Traut Kabeto

When the Blackbird Called – a book of poetry

Tales from Bohemia - a translation of twenty stories from the Bohemian Forest area between Germany, Austria and the Czech Republic. The stories are about nature spirits and their interactions with people.

Crows and Other Pedestrians – a collection of personal, critical and historical essays, a travelogue to Weimar in the former East Germany, some fun crow poetry, a short story, a Christmas story and commentaries.

Weird Steffi (Call from the distant Past) Part 1 of a trilogy - a novel about life in Germany of the 1950s in a convent boarding business school for girls where Steffi meets another Stephanie who turns out to be clairvoyant.

Fanny's Flight (Call from the distant Past) part 2 of a trilogy - Stephanie has graduated and instead of working in her father's office she is stuck as housemaid to her mother and nursemaid to her younger siblings. She meets and loses Leon, she gets stranded in a big City, gets taken prisoner by East German border guards, and has constant fights on her hands, trying to assert herself at home.

Dagobert (Call from the distant Past) is the third book of the trilogy.

Run Away Jamie – a novel for children about an unhappy girl who wants to run away from home, which is a small farm in Yakima county, Washington. Her deep psychic connection to her dead grandmother helps her cope with life, especially when her world is turned upside down.

How the Mouse Spoiled Everything and Other Stories - a chapter book for children about one family, whose eldest daughter has ESP and the problem it causes her. The stories are spread over several years.

.